THE SCHOOL FOR MYSTERIES

By Carolyn Jourdan

In this book Smoky Mountain dialect is rendered as it sounds. Appalachian speech is poetic and musical. It's sung as much as spoken, so a significant portion of the meaning is conveyed in the cadences and tones.

Dialect is used in conversation by people of all levels of education and intelligence, so no apostrophes will highlight dropped g's or word variants, as if they are errors. For the same reason, the local grammar is retained.

This was done to enable the reader to experience Smoky Mountain life and language intimately, as an insider would.

This is a work of fiction. Real places or real persons are sometimes mentioned but the story is a work of the author's imagination.

ISBN – 13: 978-0-9899304-7-5

Printed in the United States of America

Designed by Karen Key

Cover by Bran Rogers
www.postmodernobody.org

PROLOGUE

Camilla gave Phoebe hope.

Like most females her age, ever since she'd learned to read, Phoebe had used the skill to follow the gossip about Prince Charles' girlfriends. She'd watched the media arcs for Camilla and then Lady Diana as the press milked the drama for decades taking each of the women around in a circle from saint to sinner to psycho and back again.

Camilla had started out by being cast in the role of slutty girlfriend to the young Prince of Wales. She'd progressed from there to manipulative adulterer, and then conniving homewrecker—and even murderer if you read the wildest of the grief-stricken ranting on the royal forums following Diana's death.

But in the end, she'd emerged as the chic and happy Duchess of Cornwall. The fact that it had taken the Duchess thirty-five years to sort out her relationship was inspiring because at this point Phoebe had been dating for forty years. If Camilla could end up happy with a guy who was going to be a king, Phoebe figured she might still be able to realistically hold out the hope of finding her prince, too, although she didn't want a literal one.

Phoebe despised bad manners, poor hygiene, and cheating or lying. She would break off a relationship at the first indication of dishonesty or incivility. She left anyone who shouted at her or called her a name before they could finish their sentence. Sometimes that took ten years, sometimes it took ten minutes.

And the fresh hell of dating in your fifties was that, at this age, boyfriends could actually *die*. This had happened to Phoebe recently. It terrified her that at this age you couldn't even rely on men to stay alive.

Dating in middle age was strange in so many ways. It was mortifying to date someone who only knew you in your post-menopausal form. Phoebe always wished her prospective dates could've seen her when she was young, and thin, and gorgeous. That was one of the best things about having Camilla as a role model. She'd never been conventionally glamorous or beautiful, and now she was overweight and older than her husband.

This was heartening to Phoebe and to the hundreds of millions of other women around the world who wore clothing with sizes in the double digits. Phoebe wasn't sure why, but nowadays you weren't supposed to have *any* digits whatsoever, unless zero qualified as a digit.

What did size *zero* even mean? That you weren't actually there? That no fabric at all was required to make your clothes?

Seeing the new Camilla after the dentists, dermatologists, hairdressers, makeup artists, and British Vogue had all had a go at her was a game-changer. She looked downright pretty. Throw enough money—allegedly a quarter of a million dollars a year—onto a woman and *voila*!

One of the happiest moments of Phoebe's life had been seeing how perfectly gorgeous and genuinely happy the new duchess looked when she came out of the church after her wedding, wearing that stunning long blue-gray coat dress and ethereal feathered coronet.

She'd been radiant. It was a moment that changed Phoebe's life.

Now she knew for sure. *Anything* was possible.

CHAPTER 1

Phoebe clung to the side of the huge tree with all her strength. She couldn't believe she'd been talked into climbing this high.

"Don't you just love this view?" said Ivy. "It's like we have our own private balcony on the tenth floor of the world's most exclusive hotel."

Phoebe hadn't taken in the view yet, beyond the bark of the tree she was hugging. *I'm ten stories up in the air,* Phoebe thought to herself. *Why?*

Ivy Iverson, Phoebe's friend, was in her element. She was a medicinal plants expert who climbed trees for a living, researching rare species that grew high in the canopy of the rainforests and cloudforests of the Great Smoky Mountains.

Phoebe, a home health care nurse, was a lot happier at ground level. She had a phobia of heights.

"Come on, let go of the tree," Ivy urged. "You can't possibly fall. You're wearing a harness and you're still roped in, so you're perfectly safe. Come on out here and sit with me."

Phoebe peeked around the tree trunk with one eye and saw Ivy sitting on the cobweb of ropes she'd rigged so she could work up in the top of the trees. The rope *platform*, as Ivy referred to it, was a bit like the net a trapeze artist might fall into, except it was way up in the air, woven among the branches of several leviathan hemlocks.

Phoebe wanted to calm down, but she couldn't, and she couldn't make herself let go of the tree.

It was Sunday morning and Phoebe had woken up feeling old. She was fifty-eight, teetering on the border between middle-age and old-age.

Despite her best efforts to suppress them, thoughts had been recurring lately that whatever dreams of adventure she'd ever entertained, she'd better check them off the list quickly before she couldn't do anything at all except sit around and grumble about her aches and pains and yammer about her most recent visit to the doctor.

Dark thoughts like these had multiplied since she'd lost her job a couple of weeks earlier. Her work with Southern Appalachian Home Health Care hadn't paid much, but she'd loved her patients and it had given her places to go, people to see, and things to do. Now she had nowhere and nothing.

For most of the three days since the company had closed, she'd lain in bed, staring at the ceiling, wondering how she could survive. Then, this morning, she'd finally gotten bored enough to get up.

She'd heaved her legs over the side of the bed and sat there for a few minutes, imagining where she might go to look for another job. At her age, in this economy and in this part of Appalachia, her prospects were extremely grim. But it was part of Phoebe's basic nature to think positive, so she tried to count her blessings.

In one way she was glad the company she'd worked for had gone bankrupt. She'd hated Bruce, her dimwit boss, and for a couple of years her job had been in a death spiral as the company slowly collapsed on itself. But now she was a never-married, middle-aged woman with no income and no health insurance.

Then, just as she was about to fall back onto the bed in despair, the phone rang. It was her friend Ivy inviting her to go climbing. Phoebe wanted to decline for half a dozen reasons, but then she remembered the prayer Shakespeare had written for Henry V, *Not today, O Lord, O not today.*

She grabbed herself by the bootstraps and jerked—she would *not* get old *today.* She dragged herself out of bed, haphazardly ran brushes across her teeth and through her hair, dressed in layers to cope with the changes in altitude and the whimsical moisture ubiquitous to the high altitudes of the Great Smoky Mountains, and was just going out the door when the phone rang again.

She ran back into the house to answer it, hoping it was Ivy cancelling the tree climbing expedition, but it wasn't. "This is Arabella Devlin-Forrest for Ms. McFarland, please," said a woman who sounded like the Queen of England.

"This is she," said Phoebe, cautiously. Could her thoughts have actually summoned Camilla? Could the Duchess be calling her to remind her to keep her chin up? Maybe she called an old maid every day, like Richard Simmons called overweight people, to give them encouragement. This was epic.

"I'm calling on behalf of my employer to request your services as a private duty nurse. You've been very highly recommended and we were hoping that you might be able to start tomorrow morning. Would that be convenient?"

Phoebe was shocked. This was almost as good as Camilla calling her. *Thank you God*, she said to herself. At the same time she had to suppress the urge to shout, *What the hell?*

This was rural Appalachia. Very few people were rich enough to afford a private duty nurse, and nobody she'd ever heard of had a woman who sounded like the Queen to make their phone calls for them.

"Ah,…okay," Phoebe stuttered, "I think that would be okay."

The ritzy voice offered her a salary that was three times what she'd been making on her previous job and then dictated a complicated set of directions that ended with a set of GPS coordinates.

Phoebe held the phone between her ear and her shoulder, praying she wouldn't mash any buttons with her face and accidentally hang up on Mrs. Something Something-Something as she scribbled the directions on the back of an envelope she pulled out of the trash.

"You will be attending a gentleman whose privacy is of paramount importance. Therefore, as a condition of your employment, you must agree to respect his wishes that you hold all facts associated with this position in the *utmost* secrecy."

Uh,…okay, Phoebe thought to herself. This sounded like it might be a gig policing a country music star. Nowadays a lot of them were English or Australian. Her patient was probably one of them. He must've flunked out of rehab and been expelled from Nashville. If his manager sent him a couple hundred miles east, the press would leave him alone. Going to the Smokies was like falling off the face of the earth.

"Certainly," Phoebe said, mustering her most professional tone.

Most people didn't realize the profound effect geography had on Tennessee. The state was 400 miles long. It bordered eight other states, and was said to exhibit a greater variety of geological features than any other state.

Tennessee was divided into what were pompously referred to as *The Three Grand Divisions*. The segments were designated by the biggest city in the area: Memphis, Nashville, or Knoxville. Each of the three zones had a totally different culture.

Memphis, on the west end of the state, was informally known as The Capital of Mississippi. The area was flat and displayed remnants of the iconic deep-south culture. People in this area had owned slaves and made them work cotton. There was doubtless a connection between this fact and the emergence of Blues music from the region.

The instant you left Memphis, travelling to the west, you crossed a bridge over the Mississippi river and were confronted with East Arkansas. The effect was the same as if you'd just died. But if you went the other way, and drove 200 miles to the east of Memphis, you faced another sort of brutal shock—Nashville.

Most Tennesseans didn't consider Nashville to be part of their state. It was more like a place where an alien space ship had landed and offloaded a strange new race of invaders who tried to ape the local culture while simultaneously despising any actual indigenous persons they encountered.

About 200 miles east of Nashville, was Knoxville. To get from Nashville to Knoxville you first dropped off a high plateau and a spectacular escarpment and then started a long slow climb into the Great Smoky Mountains. Tennessee was not one of the ritzy states. It had a scruffy sort of image. One of the favorite sayings of Tennesseans was *Thank God for Alabama* [or *Mississippi*].

But then, when the state's indigenous music was found to be extremely lucrative worldwide—the west end for blues and the east end for bluegrass and country music—foreign hordes descended on it like the Spaniards on South American gold. From the center they figured they could manage both ends. So now Nashville was filled with people who were from *out of town*.

Sending some urban castoff faux hillbilly musician two hundred miles east of Nashville to the stark, stoic, hyper-polite, hyper-violent, hardcore Appalachian culture of the Smokies would be much worse than sending him to lockdown rehab. It would be the equivalent of sending him to hell.

Poor guy, Phoebe thought.

CHAPTER 2

It was amazing how your life could turn on a dime, even when you least expected it. One minute you were a hopeless, penniless spinster, and the next you had a great job and were sitting on a rope net a hundred feet in the air.

Phoebe had finally decided to let go of the tree and sit with her friend. Ivy was right, the view was amazing. The women sat side-by side and listened to the bird sounds and the wind in the trees.

They huffed the evergreen resin and the earthy leaf litter and enjoyed the magical *islands in the sky* view of the Smokies. It was the special treat you got when you were above a blanket of clouds that totally concealed the lower elevations and only the tips of the tallest peaks poked through. The women gazed at what seemed to be a chain of steep, forested islands separated by a sea of playful, turbulent, white mist.

"Okay, spill," Ivy said, "What changed? Why'd you finally agree to come up here with me."

"You don't understand what it's like to age," Phoebe said. "When you're young, like you are now, you think it'll go on forever. Of course you do. It's all you've ever known.

"But then years pass and one day you realize that you're not just getting older, but you're getting *old*. You can't see or hear as well as you used to. You've gotten out of shape and can't remember when that could've happened. It's so gradual you don't notice it. You see old people all around you all your life, but it still doesn't really enter your mind that every one of them used to be young and fresh and energetic and smiling. And before you know it, you're looking in the mirror at sagging jowls and loose skin flapping where your triceps used to be, wondering what the heck happened."

Ivy smiled with sympathy.

"When Sean died, it really took something out of me. It's indescribably strange to look down into a coffin and see a body that a few days ago was your boyfriend. I wasn't prepared for what that felt like. It was terrible.

"It took awhile, but I finally was starting to feel like myself again—and then I lost my job. That was a real blow because in this economy, at my age, I knew I might never find another one unless I'd work at a fast food place."

Ivy leaned against Phoebe and rested her head on her friend's shoulder.

"I felt afraid for the first time in my life. But then I reminded myself of the Duchess of Cornwall and the odds she overcame. *Gee*, talk about your long shots."

Ivy had no idea who the Duchess of Cornwall was, but she was embarrassed to admit it, since the woman was obviously very important to Phoebe.

"Because of her," Phoebe said, "I know I'll always have a chance to start my life over again and create whatever kind of life want. I decided to start today by facing my fear of heights. I knew if I could climb up here, I could do anything."

The women smiled at each other.

"What's going on with you and Henry?" Ivy asked.

Henry and Phoebe were childhood friends who'd recently come into contact with each other again. The small community of White Oak was watching them carefully for any signs of romance.

"He's in California right now," Phoebe said, "fighting a wildfire. He and a bunch of other rangers volunteered and they're out there for who knows how long. I guess until they get the fire out."

"That's not what I meant," said Ivy.

Phoebe took a deep breath. "I don't have the same kind of romantic motivation I used to have when I was younger. It may be partially hormonal. Post-menopause is *such* a relief. You don't realize how much of your decision-making is affected by hormones until they go away.

"Then, all of a sudden, it's like you get your brain back, except it's not *back* because you've never actually had it before. It's more like you finally notice you have a brain in the first place. It makes you feel sorry for yourself, having been brainless for your whole life up until now without ever realizing it.

"It's not like I haven't tried to participate in all the social norms. I've been dating for four decades now, that's a bunch of guys. But from what I've seen romance is massively over-rated. It's a dangerous delusion."

Ivy poked Phoebe with her elbow. "Come on," she said.

"What I'm trying to say is that I've learned from dating longer than you've been alive that *friendship* is real, but what's commonly meant by the word *romance* isn't," Phoebe explained. "These days I'm looking for a friend, someone fun to travel with, or go to the movies or eat out with, but not a husband. I was never looking for a husband. I was always looking for a decent, reliable buddy.

"You know the first people Dante ran into on his trip to hell were a romantic couple totally wrapped up in each other. They were locked in a whirlwind together. Dante *fainted* when he saw what they were reaping as a result of their so-called *romance*."

Phoebe knew Ivy was too young to care about things like this. She was still in thrall to youth, and that was understandable and right. But she'd asked, so Phoebe had given her something to think about.

"Enough about men," Phoebe said. "I have some really great news. I've been saved! I got a job this morning. It starts tomorrow. Just one patient and a whole lot of money."

She told Ivy about the phone call and her friend congratulated her. Then they sat in companionable silence, enjoying the view together. "You're right," Phoebe said. "This place really is paradise.

CHAPTER 3

The sound of wind rustling through the leaves was being progressively drowned out by a rhythmical thumping that was gaining volume. At first Phoebe thought it was the beating of her own heart. She wondered if it was palpitations or if she was about to have a panic attack from the height. Maybe the exertion of the climb was bringing on a heart attack. Then she realized it was a helicopter approaching. That was strange. She knew it wouldn't be tourists because this area of the Smokies was famous for deadly wind shears. They were called *orographic lifts*, and they could be over a hundred miles an hour.

It was a local phenomenon caused by the Smokies being the first major windbreak between the Atlantic Ocean and the rest of the country. So many aircraft had crashed because of these notorious winds, authorities were extremely reluctant to send any air rescue to the area, even in the most dire emergencies. There was no point in adding to the body count.

Injured people were frequently airlifted from other areas of the National Park and taken to a hospital in Knoxville. It was much faster than an ambulance on account of the distance and the dense, slow-moving traffic that surrounded the nation's top family vacation destination. More than nine million tourists a year visited the Park. That made for hideous traffic.

The helicopter sound was getting *very* loud. The two women couldn't help but look up even though the dense vegetation meant they'd get a quick glimpse at most, and that only if the chopper passed directly overhead. But then suddenly, there it was.

Before Phoebe could even register what she was seeing, a large pale form flashed into her field of vision, fell toward her, and hit the net she and Ivy were sitting on with a powerful impact.

She reflexively grabbed Ivy's arm to help keep her balance as the platform recoiled like a trampoline. The two women were able to keep their seats, but just barely. They turned together to look behind them and were astonished at the figure that lay there, splayed out. It was the body of a man, naked, lying face up, draped bonelessly across the rope netting.

Had the body blown out of a stretcher mounted on the side of the helicopter?

Had it fallen out of the helicopter itself?

Ivy was immediately on her feet. She glanced at Phoebe and said, "Did you see that? It looked almost like those guys *threw* him out the door of that helicopter!"

No, Phoebe hadn't seen it, but her eyes weren't that good anymore. Her focal length no longer transitioned smoothly. She needed at least four pairs of glasses to make it these days—reading, computing, driving, and sunglasses. She didn't have any lenses for viewing low-flying aircraft.

But rather than heading toward the body, Ivy moved even farther away from it. As gracefully as an acrobat, she walked along the network of ropes until she was as far away as she could possibly get. She stood against a tree trunk, staring at the dead man in horror. She'd never seen a dead body before.

Phoebe was a bit surprised that Ivy wouldn't try to render assistance, but fear of a body was common. Most people moved away from death or trouble. Fortunately people like doctors, soldiers, policemen, and firefighters tended to have the opposite impulse.

Phoebe looked at the body and noted that the man's face was still a healthy pink. He hadn't been dead long. Then the corpse coughed.

Oh God, she thought, *he's not quite dead. Yet.*

Phoebe recognized the sound for what it was and began an awkward crawl across the net toward the man. He was vomiting while lying on his back. He was choking. She made it to the middle of the net and shoved him over onto his side so he wouldn't drown in his own vomit.

The two men standing in the open doorway of the helicopter exchanged surprised looks and spoke to each other via their helmet microphones at the same time. One said, "What was that?" and the other, "Did you see that?"

The taller man wore a harness with a tether connected to a hook in the ceiling of the chopper. He leaned out as far as he could and scanned the forest below them.

"I saw something," said the tall guy. "It could've been a person."

"There was some sort of tree stand," said the other man, "I couldn't tell what it was."

"Do you think someone saw us?" said the tall man.

"Let's go find out."

The shorter fellow instructed the pilot to turn around immediately and retrace his route. Both men grabbed handholds to keep from falling out the door as the chopper tilted and wheeled around.

Phoebe had no idea what condition the man was in. He had to have been injured, but his color was decent and he was still warm. She felt for a pulse. It was sky high, but that was understandable. He'd just endured a free fall without the benefit of a parachute or even a pair of boxer shorts.

"Can you hear me?" she asked in a gentle voice.

He moaned.

"You've had an accident," she said, "but you're safe now."

His eyes fluttered open. His pupils looked good. They were even and reactive to light. She could tell he was trying to focus on her, but was having trouble. She held up two fingers and said, "Can you tell me how many fingers I'm holding up?"

His eyes closed and he didn't respond.

When he started retching again, Phoebe steadied him, keeping him on his side. She had no way of knowing if he had any broken bones or internal injuries, but the vomiting was ominous. He might've damaged something in his abdomen or hurt his head.

"It's okay now," she lied, "Everything will be okay now. I've gotcha."

The sound of the helicopter started getting louder again. It must be coming back.

The man was mumbling. Phoebe leaned close to try to hear what he was saying. His deep throated growl was hard to understand but it sounded like, "Not *them* again."

Suddenly the chopper was overhead, and this time it stayed there for several seconds, hovering. Two men wearing helmets, black jumpsuits, and heavy black boots were standing in the open door looking down at Phoebe and her new patient. They were right out in the middle of the rope platform in plain sight. Ivy was still standing with her back against the tree trunk, which meant she was well hidden from above.

The fallen man recoiled in terror against the wind being whipped up by the helicopter blades. The men in the chopper had to be able to see that he was moving under his own power. Phoebe squinted up through the flying bits of leaves and her lashing hair and wondered if that was a good thing, or a bad thing.

The wind was buffeting the chopper. It was gusting and shoving it hard toward the ridge and into the tops of the trees. The pilot couldn't hold their position for more than a few seconds before he was forced to move away from the wall of mountains.

But they'd seen enough. Loose ends would have to be dealt with, pronto.

CHAPTER 4

The helicopter noise faded and this time it didn't come back.

Phoebe's vision wasn't great, but she'd seen enough to confirm that the helicopter wasn't one of the types used for medical rescue. It wasn't rigged with a basket on the side for transport of a body, either. This wasn't adding up.

"That was super-weird," Ivy said, "Those guys didn't wave or anything. They just looked."

The man mumbled again, still keeping his eyes closed tightly, but this time he was easier to understand. He said, "Uh oh."

The guy really had a knack for hitting the nail on the head. He was a man of few words, but every one of them was right on target.

Phoebe was getting a cramp from kneeling on the ropes. She needed to change position. "I'm gonna lay you over on your stomach for just a second," she said. His eyelids fluttered open just as she rolled him facedown.

"Oh God!" he gasped, and flailed his arms and legs wildly. Then he screamed.

Phoebe threw herself across him to keep him from thrashing and flinging himself off the edge of the platform in his frenzy. "Stop that!" Phoebe barked. "Stop it right now!"

"It's not over," he moaned. "I'm still falling!"

"Close your eyes," Phoebe said in her most authoritative voice. "You are *not* falling."

"Uhhhh," he groaned, but he closed his eyes, then whispered, "That's better."

Ivy and Phoebe exchanged concerned looks.

After a couple of minutes his breathing became more regular and, he asked in a husky voice, "Am I dead?"

"No," said Phoebe. "I'm gonna get off you now. I need you to roll back up onto your side when I do that, okay? Keep your eyes closed and just roll onto your side. I'll help you. Don't try to go anywhere else."

When she lifted herself off him he made an ungentlemanly grunt like she weighed a ton. She held him in a firm grip and leaned in close to check his pupils, as she said, "I need to take a quick look at your eyes. Hold still."

When she pried open one of his eyelids he looked up into Phoebe's face at nearly point blank range, and shouted, "Oh God, I'm in Hell!"

Phoebe was used to verbal abuse from patients. She knew people weren't at their best when they were sick, scared, in pain, or heavily medicated, but Ivy was shocked and wouldn't stand for this stranger insulting her friend.

"Hey, buddy, watch your mouth. We're trying to help you," Ivy said, pulling off her fleece jacket and tossing it toward his private parts. "And cover up, you're not exactly Chippendales material yourself."

Phoebe snorted. She didn't mind his outburst. Some people were just bad patients. No matter what you did for them they were cranky and a pain in the ass to deal with. This fellow was obviously one of those.

"I've heard of people getting bumped from a flight," Ivy said, still miffed at him, "but you just took it to a whole new level."

That made him cough and sputter in what might have been a laugh.

"If you keep you eyes closed it'll help you stay calm," Phoebe said. The height was scaring her, too. "We'll figure out a way to get you down."

"Who *are* you people?" he asked in a hoarse whisper.

"Who are *you*?" Ivy demanded.

He mumbled, "I asked first."

As the helicopter left the mountains, the shorter of the two men said, "The boss isn't gonna like this."

"What say we clean up the mess ourselves and not mention it to him?"

"Agreed," he said. No one would ever want to have to admit a mistake to the man they knew only as the Gryphon.

They radioed their associates, described the situation, requested emergency ground-based assistance, and relayed the precise GPS coordinates of the body drop.

"Yeah, retrieval and secure disposal," the tall guy said, "Of the target and any and all subjects in the area. We have a female witness."

He listened to the response, then said, "Thanks. I owe you one," before terminating the connection.

What a crazy day. It had started out as a typical job. They'd snatched some geek from his basement in Cleveland, cleaned the place, and torched it. Then they'd taken him five hundred miles south, stripped him of all identification, and tossed him out of the chopper to kill him and get rid of the body in one fell swoop, so to speak. Why do the extra labor of burying some schmuck if you didn't have to?

And then what? The guy didn't die from the fall! How had that happened?

Things were really crazy when you couldn't even toss a guy out in mid-air and be sure he'd end up dead. It made no sense. Somehow they'd thrown the nerd out onto the few square feet he could've landed on that wouldn't have killed him outright.

That was some freakin guardian angel he had.

CHAPTER 5

"Are you saying that he didn't fall? That this wasn't an accident?" Phoebe asked.

"I don't think it was," Ivy said.

"You think they *threw* him out? Of a helicopter?"

Ivy nodded reluctantly.

"Why?"

Ivy shrugged. "Where are his clothes?"

Phoebe looked down at him to confirm the absence of clothing. She was so used to working with people in various states of undress that she hadn't thought about it. "I've read that in air disasters, when people fall from a great height, their clothes, even their underwear, usually get blown off during the fall. But, I don't think he fell far enough for that to have happened."

"Maybe he's a terrorist or a criminal who'd just been arrested and strip-searched," Ivy said. "Or if they're bad guys, they could've been trying to remove any identification before killing him. They always do that on the television shows."

The women looked at him. "Or maybe he just pissed somebody

off. Who knows?"

"He knows," Phoebe said.

He shook his head slowly, denying it.

"Do you think they saw us?" Phoebe asked.

"I think they must've seen something right after they tossed him out," Ivy said, "and then, when they came back, they saw you both. I doubt if they saw me, though."

"Do you think they figured out that he's not dead?"

"He was obviously moving, so they've got to be worried that he's still alive."

"Do you think they'll come after us?"

"If they're good people, they'll come back to help him. If they're bad guys they apparently want him dead and I doubt they want any witnesses. So it's not just him they're after now. It doesn't seem likely that they'd just give up. People who have the resources to use a helicopter are professionals. I think all three of us better get outta here as quick as we can."

Neither of them said anything, but the two women looked at the stranger, wondering what they could do with him.

"Oh don't worry about me," he said, in a sarcastic tone, "I'll be fine."

"I might be able to get him down using your harness," said Ivy. "But I'm not sure. He might be too heavy for me to handle."

"I don't know if we can move him out of here in a harness without seriously exacerbating his injuries," Phoebe said.

"If we leave him, his injuries are going to get exacerbated at lot more. Let's go get Leon," Ivy suggested. "He can get him down."

Phoebe thought about it and nodded in agreement. Leon was Ivy's boyfriend and he taught climbing at Cloud Forest, the local posh resort.

Ivy walked toward the edge of the platform and said, "Let's go."

"I'll stay here with our mystery man," Phoebe said. "It's not safe to leave him up here alone."

"It's not safe for you to stay here with him, either, but I know better than to argue with you," Ivy said. "I'll be back as quick as I can."

She checked her gear then stepped off the platform and zipped down toward the ground so fast it made Phoebe dizzy. Ivy was *burning a rope* as the climbers called it when their descent was so fast the friction of the equipment heated the rope enough to melt it, not to mention what it did to a glove—and the hand inside it.

The second her feet touched the ground Ivy stepped out of her harness and took off running through the forest toward her car.

Phoebe crawled to the man's feet and began a careful examination of her patient. She straightened his legs, put his ankles together, and checked to see that both legs were the same length and that neither foot rotated outwards more than normal. They looked fine, so he hadn't broken a hip. She felt along the big bone in each of his lower legs to make sure he hadn't broken a tibia.

Then she pressed against the skin on his thighs. Both thighs were warm, but not hot, and not abnormally hard to the touch, so he hadn't broken a femur. If he had, at least a pint of blood would've leaked into the surrounding area and caused palpable heat and skin tightness from the swelling.

She crawled toward his upper body and examined his arms, shoulders, and chest. By some miracle, he didn't have any noticeable injuries that looked life-threatening, but of course, there were all sorts of terrible possibilities she couldn't see, a ruptured spleen, for one—the list was too long to contemplate.

She sat back on her heels and looked at him. He looked a little taller than she was, so she guessed he was maybe six feet. He was muscular, but the muscles were the normal flat kind, not the bulging ones that were the latest craze. Phoebe crawled up toward his head and felt around on his scalp. It was dry. He hadn't cut his head and she didn't feel any depressions in his skull.

He looked to be about her age, in his fifties. There was silver mixed in with brown in his wild halo of curls. His hair was clean and soft, longer than normal for someone his age, but she didn't know if that was due to vanity or simply a failure to get frequent haircuts.

He hadn't made any sounds during the exam, but she knew he was conscious because he was smiling.

"Don't stop," he said. "I'm trying to enjoy this. I haven't been naked around a woman in a long time."

"I'm very glad you're alive, but try not to get carried away."

"Honey, the shape I'm in, if I don't get carried, I'm not going anywhere at all."

He was funny, even when he was in pain. That told Phoebe a lot about his character.

"What's your name?" she asked.

He didn't answer right away, but when Phoebe didn't press him, he finally mumbled, "Nick."

"My name's Phoebe. That was Ivy who just left to get help so we can get you down from here. Can you tell me what happened?"

"I fell."

"We got that part," Phoebe said. "Was it an accident?"

There was a pause, then he murmured, "No."

CHAPTER 6

"Why would someone do that to you?"

This time the pause was even longer, and he shifted slightly before answering. He was obviously in pain when he said, "I guess I made em mad."

"Are they the mafia?"

He barked a short laugh, and that started him coughing. Phoebe held his hand until he quieted.

"Who are they?" she asked.

"Didn't introduce themselves."

"What did you do that made someone mad enough to kill you?"

His brow furrowed, "My research...maybe."

Phoebe didn't say anything, hoping he'd continue, but if he didn't she wouldn't press him. His lack of clothing prevented her from getting any clues about him that way, but he had no tattoos or scars except for an old straight line cut just underneath his chin. That was a scar nearly every active little boy got at some point. There were no surgical scars and no suspicious marks like from knife wounds or bullet holes. She decided he didn't look like a criminal.

She could tell he was gradually settling down, but he was still keeping his eyes tightly closed. She wondered if he was simply afraid of heights, like her, or if he was seeing double or had vertigo. "I need to check your vision again," she said, as she touched his face and began to peel back an eyelid.

"No!" he said, and knocked her arm away.

"What's wrong?"

He breathed several deep breaths and let them out through his nose before saying, "I have some … issues. Serious issues."

She waited to hear what they were, but he remained quiet.

"What sort of issues?"

"Agoraphobia," he whispered, like even the word scared him.

Ohhhh, that explained a lot. This was what the helicopter had been about. Torture. How horrible to have been swept out of his safe place and tossed out into the wild blue yonder. It was the worst possible thing they could've done to him. Someone must really hate him.

"Okay," she said, "I understand." His fear of wide spaces might've been what caused the vomiting. If he was bleeding into his brain, and she saw one or both of his pupils become fixed, there was nothing she could do about it anyway, so she wouldn't pry his eyes open again. She took off the fleece headband she used to hold her hair back.

She told him what she was going to do, then put it around his head and over his eyes like a blindfold. She'd seen her ranger friend Henry do something similar to wild animals when he was working on them. He said it was a kindness that helped them stay calm, like a hood for a falcon.

The man's breathing slowed and his heart rate came down after that.

"What were you researching?" she asked.

He took a deep breath and swallowed audibly. She could tell he was waiting for nausea to subside, then he said, "The cause of war."

Wow, she hadn't seen that coming. She knew it was likely that he was still a bit addled. A fall like that would temporarily scramble anyone's brains.

"Why would that make anybody mad?" she asked.

"They don't want … wars to stop."

"Oh," Phoebe said, "the military-industrial complex."

He laughed again, and started retching. Phoebe rolled him onto his side and held him steady until the gagging subsided. "Who do you think it is?"

"It's complicated," he sighed, "It could be anybody."

Phoebe wondered if he was crazy, or if this was evidence of a head injury that was getting worse, but then she remembered he'd been shoved out of a helicopter. That certainly leant credence to any outlandish story he might come out with.

After something like that you couldn't blame a guy for feeling paranoid. She didn't ask him any more questions, though, because talking was difficult for him. There'd be plenty of time to sort things out later.

She sat with him in silence, contemplating the situation. The scene was like something out of a religious painting or *Paradise Lost*. A man had fallen out of the sky and nearly into her lap. She briefly entertained the notion that he might be an angel, but then realized the cynical and sarcastic tone of his few utterances would seem to indicate a fallen angel at best.

Phoebe knew her Bible. She knew that Lucifer had gotten himself cast out of heaven and that he was said to be the most beautiful of all the angels. She looked at the man carefully. She hadn't really noticed before because she was worried about him, but he was kinda gorgeous.

Since his eyes were closed, she was free to admire his charmingly disheveled hair, dark eyebrows, straight nose, and long thick dark eyelashes. She tried to remember the color of his eyes, but she hadn't gotten much of a look. He seemed to be sleeping. That was either a good thing, or not.

Neither of them spoke again as they waited for Ivy to return, but Phoebe kept a close watch over Nick. And she prayed. The image of Lucifer wouldn't go away, though, so at one point she stopped, worried that she might praying for the Devil.

Then she started back up again, thinking that the Devil probably needed our prayers most of all.

CHAPTER 7

Phoebe heard rustling in the forest. Someone was coming.

Then she heard the snapping of twigs underfoot. Whoever it was, they were getting closer. She could tell Nick heard it too, because he tightened his grip on the rope net. She put a hand on his shoulder to reassure him, and removed his blindfold, but neither of them made a sound.

Tense seconds ticked by with more noises of someone or something crashing through the dense vegetation nearby, then Ivy and Leon emerged. Neither of them spoke. They made hand signals to Phoebe, and remained silent as they rigged their gear.

Leon tilted a crossbow up, needing to shoot a guide line for his climbing rope. Phoebe understood what he as doing and kept a steady hand on Nick to keep him from freaking out if he should open his eyes and see the weapon.

Leon aimed at a sturdy limb above the research platform and signaled that Phoebe should duck her head so he could shoot. She crouched down next to Nick and whispered, "It's okay."

Leon and Ivy and made their ascent as quickly and quietly as possible and knelt beside Phoebe and Nick. They whispered that they'd heard some other people in the area. They hadn't been able to see them, so they didn't know who they were, but the implications were obvious. Ivy's research area was pretty far off the beaten track, so there was a strong possibility it was the helicopter people looking to finish their job.

"Stay quiet," Leon whispered to Nick, "and do what I tell you. Don't worry, I'll have you down from here in a minute." Then he turned to Phoebe and whispered, "As soon as we hit the ground, we'll go for my truck instead of your Jeep. It's farther away, but it's hidden. It's on the old logging road where the poachers like to park. I'm afraid people might've seen your Jeep. Anyone coming in here would've had to pass it."

Phoebe knew the place Leon was talking about. She nodded her understanding.

He pointed at Nick and said, "I'll carry him."

Leon dressed Nick in a pair of baggy cargo shorts and a ragged t-shirt. Then he helped him sit up and put the climbing harness on him.

He clipped Nick's harness to his own and said softly, "You don't have to do anything. Just stay still, and whatever you do, don't pull on this knot."

He indicated the Blake's Hitch, the complex knot that would allow them to control their descent and would work as dead man's switch to arrest their fall if necessary, "Don't touch this."

Nick slitted one eye open just enough to glance at the knot warily.

"Don't touch any of the ropes, understand?"

Nick nodded.

Leon scooted to the edge of the platform and he and Ivy half-dragged Nick until they had him seated next to Leon. When both men had their legs dangling over the edge, Phoebe touched his shoulder and whispered, "Keep your eyes closed."

He was obviously in pain and Phoebe knew he must be horribly nauseous and afraid, but he didn't make a sound. Phoebe had seen a lot of sick and injured people and knew how they behaved. This guy was one very tough cookie. She couldn't help but be impressed.

Leon pushed himself over the edge and dragged Nick with him. Then they started down. When they touched down, Nick's legs wouldn't support him, so Leon held him in a big bear hug.

Ivy waited until the men were on the ground, then she rigged Phoebe's harness and attached it to hers and the women made the same type of descent the guys had just made. Phoebe had never rappelled before. It felt sort of like being on an elevator, except without the floor or walls or ceiling, and the elevator swayed in three dimensions. She took the same advice she'd given Nick and kept her eyes closed.

Despite everything that had happened, she had a nearly irresistible urge to yodel like Tarzan on the way down, but in consideration of their safety, she didn't give in to the impulse. It was amazing how fear was relative. Being chased by professional assassins had dampened Phoebe's concerns about getting to the ground.

At least she had a rope.

By the time all four of them were on the ground they could easily hear people thrashing around nearby. It sounded like more than one person. They shucked out of their harnesses as quietly as possible and left the long ropes dangling.

Leon handed Phoebe the keys to his truck and gestured that she should give him her keys. She handed them to him. He pointed to an ancient tree that had fallen over and whispered into her ear, using a cupped hand to cover any sounds, "Ya'll hide in the hole under the big stump.

"Go, now. Ivy and I'll lead these fellows away. We'll take em over toward Sanderson's Hell. Then we'll come back and get your Jeep and meet you at the café." Then he began removing his shoes.

A *hell* was the local term for an impenetrable thicket of briars created by mountain laurel and rhododendron roots and branches. These areas were common in the Smokies. They could be found in small patches or they might cover large areas. They were impossible to navigate in or through. If you could traverse them at all, it was exhausting, and you'd get lost because you couldn't maintain a straight line of movement.

Nick was so weak Phoebe could barely support him. He was as pale as death, too. She was concerned that the rappelling had worsened his situation. She gestured toward her patient and mouthed one word to Leon, *hospital.*

Leon nodded and pulled his shirt off over his head. Then he began to unzip his jeans. He twirled his finger to indicate that Phoebe should turn around. She did and then she helped Nick hobble toward the dark cavity created by the rotting tree. She helped him sit down and then scoot back underneath the huge fallen log. She quickly brushed damp leaves over his legs, then sat beside him and did the same for herself.

She glanced around in time to see a flash of the pale form of Leon undressed, pretending to limp away with Ivy's assistance. Within seconds the couple disappeared in that disconcerting way that was so easy to do in the lush vegetation of the cloudforest.

Almost immediately she heard sounds close by, approaching from another direction. Two figures moved by wearing camouflage. It was clear that the men were professionals. They moved carefully, and wore an array of gear strapped all over themselves that Phoebe couldn't begin to identify.

The men crept off in the direction Leon and Ivy had gone.

Phoebe was frightened for her friends. She could feel Nick shivering beside her, from shock, fear, cold, or maybe all three. She didn't move a muscle because her ranger friend Henry had taught her that it was movement, more than anything else, that made it possible to spot people or animals in the forest. He'd said that if a person would hold still, they'd be nearly impossible to see, even if they weren't wearing camo.

She trusted Henry and knew he was an expert in woodscraft. He'd learned the trick of stillness from hunting and also from his work with rescue teams. She knew people who were unconscious or dead were extremely hard to locate in the wilderness. He'd lamented how many times searchers had walked right by a body, even one dressed in bright-colored clothing, without ever realizing it.

Leon and Henry's advice worked. The two pursuers moved past Phoebe and Nick's hiding place and continued to move away until they couldn't be heard any more.

Phoebe and Nick remained hidden under the tree roots for a couple more minutes until she figured the bad guys were well away from them. Then she stood, helped Nick up, and supported him as much as she could as they made their way through the forest, heading for Leon's truck.

CHAPTER 8

Leon and Ivy were moving quickly, but leaving a trail that was pretty obvious. It was a good thing they were dating, Leon thought. He wouldn't have wanted to run through the woods in his birthday suit with anyone besides his girlfriend. It was embarrassing to do it even with Ivy, not to mention painful.

Fortunately both of them were extremely fit and thoroughly familiar with the area. The people who were chasing them had no idea of the terrain or the vegetative nightmare that was coming. That gave Leon and Ivy a tremendous edge. An almost comical advantage, except that the people who were after them would most certainly have guns, while they had only their wits.

By unspoken agreement the couple headed toward Andrews Creek. The noisy creek would cover the sounds of their movement as they lead their pursuers into the trap and would also provide the means for them to change direction and escape.

It would be fairly simple to lay a trail that would get the bad guys stuck in a tangle of blackberry briars, rhododendron, laurel, and witch and dog hobble. But Leon and Ivy would be able to avoid the hell by doubling back and leaving the area, walking in the creek. They'd be almost impossible to track.

If the men coming after them hadn't been killers, Leon might've felt sorry for them.

Phoebe guessed it was about noon by the time she and Nick reached Leon's ancient Datsun truck. "We've got to get you to a hospital right away. I'll take you to Charlie," she said

"Who's Charlie?" Nick asked.

"A friend, and a doctor. He's a radiologist, so if I can get you to where he works, he'll be able to figure out if there's anything seriously wrong with you."

"There's *a lot* of things seriously wrong with me," Nick muttered.

Phoebe agreed, but didn't say so out loud. She turned the little truck around and took off for Knoxville.

Leon and Ivy crouched behind another of the many *blowdowns*, a full-grown tree that had been knocked onto its side by the wind. They hoped their pursuers had been able to follow them, but not too closely. Keeping an even distance between themselves and the bad guys wasn't easy.

Thank goodness they were close to the boisterous creek. Once they were sure the men chasing them had taken the bait and entered the hell, Leon and Ivy planned to use the noise of rushing water to mask the sounds of their escape. If they walked carefully in the rocky streambed, the water would conceal their tracks as well.

They'd reached the crucial point. They worked quickly to break off bits of shrubbery on both sides of the creek and lay a false trail by making deep foot impressions and slide marks on the opposite bank. Then they stepped into the middle of the stream walked away from the infamous thicket, hoping they'd be able to trick their pursuers into stumbling on into the acres and acres of shrubbery.

As they crept away, they could hear people crashing and thrashing their way into the progressively more dense laurel. Sanderson's Hell it was called. *Hell indeed*, thought Leon, *knock yourselves out, boys.*

Leon smiled to himself as he thought of the line in Brer Rabbit, *Whatever you do, don't throw me into the briar patch.*

Other men might've been reluctant to employ the tactics of a bunny rabbit to try to evade stone cold killers. But Leon was not only wise enough to use the most humble of methods to save the lives of four innocent people, including himself, but also he was secure enough in his masculinity to be able to enjoy it.

CHAPTER 9

Phoebe took the curve of the exit ramp so fast the Datsun truck hopped several times in its struggle to make the tight turn. At the bottom of the ramp she looked both ways and then ran the red light that guarded the entrance to the jumbled complex of hospital buildings. She drove to the closest parking garage and took a ramp down into the underground portion. When she was on the lowest level she stopped in front of a set of glass doors that led into a small elevator lobby.

There were no benches anywhere to be seen. That was not good. Maybe she should've gone to the Emergency entrance, but she was trying to keep a low profile—very low, subterranean, in fact.

She looked over at her passenger to make sure he was still alive. He was breathing, at least. They hadn't spoken during the drive to the hospital. He'd seemed to faint almost as soon as he got into Leon's truck. Whether it was from an injury or the shock of being forced out into wide-open spaces, she didn't know. She'd had to fasten his seatbelt for him.

Now she touched him on the shoulder to rouse him, and said, "Can you stand here while I park the car?"

"Maybe," he said in a husky voice.

His eyes opened to little slits. Phoebe registered the color for the first time. They were a beautiful clear green.

She threw the gearshift into park and ran around to let him out. She helped him hobble through the automatic doors and left him leaning against the wall in the little lobby while she ran back to the truck and drove it to a dark corner of the garage. She parked it next to a concrete pillar to hide it as well as she could.

So far so good. She was no expert, but she didn't think they'd been followed.

Nick's skin was a pale blue-gray by the time she got back to him. She hoped his pallor was due to the eerie anti-viral lights mounted on the wall and not an indication that he was bleeding to death internally.

"It's a long way to the Radiology Department," Phoebe said, as she pressed the button to the elevator. "I'm sorry."

There was a ding to signal the arrival of a car. She draped his left arm over her shoulders, and said, "Try to act as normal as possible."

He grunted and nodded, then shuffled alongside her as she moved into the elevator. They went up three floors and then moved out into a long empty corridor. At first Phoebe was surprised that no one was around and then she realized it was Sunday afternoon and this was the building that housed the offices of the various medical specialists. They were all closed today.

They slowly made their way toward the main part of the hospital. At one point they had to use a glass overpass to cross above a street. Nick shuddered the whole way across. When they approached a corridor where there were some people, he loosened his grip to a more affectionate, less desperate looking hold. But his pace slowed even more.

Phoebe realized he wasn't going to make it, so she commandeered an abandoned wheelchair left beside one of the exit doors and rolled him the rest of the way toward their destination. He sagged in the chair and Phoebe had to grab the back of his t-shirt a couple of times to keep him from falling forward into the floor.

They had to pass through the central lobby at the hospital's main entrance to get to the Radiology Department. They arrived at the automated double doors at same time a gurney was being rolled in, so they followed it inside.

Phoebe searched her brain, trying to remember how to get to Charlie's office. Nick didn't look like he had more than a few minutes left in him.

She heard someone call out behind her, "Stop!"

She knew better than to look back, but she couldn't help herself. A burley man dressed in blue jeans and a navy windbreaker was staring at her while talking into a fancy little radio. He was clearly not hospital security.

Dang, they had people watching the hospitals.

Phoebe shoved the wheelchair with all her might. She took the first turn she came to and pushed Nick at a flat out run. She couldn't keep that up for long, though. It made a spectacle for one thing. Doctors and nurses only ran and screamed and acted like lunatics on television shows. Behavior like that would be highly detrimental to a real patient's recovery.

Phoebe needed to find a place to hide until she could figure out a way to get in touch with Charlie. She took another turn and then, miraculously, she realized where she was. And she got an idea.

She mentally blessed Charlie. He was such a good friend. Who else could she go to in such a bizarre situation?

She loved the Radiology Department. She'd spent many a night sitting beside Charlie, for hours on end, watching him work. There was something so calming about his black and white world. It was the only place in the hospital where there was no color, no sound, no blood, no screaming. Here he could work all alone, in serene isolation, without any real patients ever showing up in person.

Until now.

CHAPTER 10

Phoebe's breath was coming in gasps and she was slowing down, but then she saw it—a matte black rounded protrusion from the wall. "In here!" she said.

"In *where?*" Nick asked.

"Can you stand up outta this wheelchair on your own?"

"Probably not."

"You're gonna have to do your best. I'm not strong enough to lift you by myself and they're right behind us."

"In that case, sure."

"We'll only get one try at this, so whatever you do, don't fall. *One, two, three,*" she said and then heaved and slammed Nick against the wall, pressing against him with her whole body, to keep him from falling.

"Don't you dare faint!" she gasped into his ear.

She kicked the wheelchair backwards across the hall and it came to rest in an alcove next to a rack of protective clothing for the Radiology staff.

She slid her hands between Nick and the wall until she was able to grab both her wrists and lock her arms around him.

"Sweetheart," he groaned, "everywhere you're touching me ... *hurts.*"

"Slide to the right," she said, "just a single step to the right."

"Don't worry, I like bossy women," he panted. "It's sorta fun being manhandled, as long as it's not by men."

Again he was displaying that heroic comic response to an extremely unpleasant situation. Phoebe liked this guy. And she liked his voice. It was husky, like he hadn't spoken very much for a long time.

Phoebe put her fingertips into a depression built into the curved metal that bulged out slightly into the corridor and did something that seemed to pry the wall away. Then she helped Nick move one more step to the right. She glanced across the hall one last time to confirm that the wheelchair was rolled out of sight of anyone looking down the long hallway.

"This is going to be a tight fit," she said, as she shuffled backwards into the dark space with him hugged to her. "Keep your arms and fingers inside," she warned.

"Inside what?" he asked in a slurred voice as she fumbled toward the wall again and slid a half round cover around them on a circular track. It was as if she'd swirled a big black cape around them both. The whole world went dark.

For a moment Nick thought he'd fainted, but then the gloom lightened almost imperceptibly. That made him wonder if he'd died.

If he had, he hoped he'd be seeing the light people talked about, but no more light came. That seemed like a bad sign. He groaned, but then he realized was still standing up, sort of, with Phoebe's arms clenched around him and she was yammering into his ear.

"Okay," she said, breathing heavily, "You have to step out into the room now. Watch out, there's a slight lip on the track for the door."

"Where are we?" he mumbled.

"The darkroom."

"Good name for it."

"It's not used any more," Phoebe said. "Things are digital now. They don't develop film in trays these days. Nobody will find us in here. Nobody would even think to look. Only the old-timers know this room exists."

Nick's eyes were adjusting to the deep gloom and he could barely make out a small room, maybe ten feet square, with waist-high counters lining three walls. A jumble of metal trays and various incomprehensible tools and gadgets were piled around. It was extremely dusty.

"I need to sit down," he said, and promptly fell to the floor.

"Don't do that!" Phoebe said. "You'll hurt yourself!"

She crouched beside him, "You coulda hit your head!" she scolded. "If you're gonna faint, the least you can do is protect your head when you fall."

He didn't respond. He might've swooned into unconsciousness again. She sighed and felt for his face and brushed his hair off his forehead. Then she felt around on the back of his head. His hair was still dry. Good, he hadn't cut his scalp.

She sat down beside him and tried to think what to do next. "You're right," she said, talking into the darkness, "you're better off in the floor for now. Nothing else can possibly happen to you if you stay down here."

"Don't you believe it," he mumbled.

She couldn't see his face, but she could tell from his voice that he was trying to smile. Phoebe wasn't used to so much exertion. She was worn out. She lay down next to him on the dusty floor and, without meaning to, fell into an exhausted slumber.

Once they were certain the bait had been taken and their adversaries were well and truly ensnared in Sanderson's Hell, Leon and Ivy carefully circled back.

They approached Phoebe's Jeep with the utmost stealth. Fortunately no one was waiting for them there. They were able to retrieve the vehicle and drive to Hamilton's Store to await Phoebe's call.

They wolfed down grilled cheeses and sweet tea the owner, Phoebe's good friend Jill, set before them. They briefed her and café regular, Doc, the retired local doctor who'd mentored Phoebe all her life.

It was a deeply worrisome situation, but all they could do was wait for Phoebe to contact them.

"We've lost them," the man in the windbreaker said into his radio. "We know they're in here somewhere in the hospital, though. So it's just a matter of time until we find them." He pretended more confidence than he felt.

He liked knowing their quarry was injured seriously enough to need to come here. But the place was enormous, a labyrinth of halls that wound above and below ground among half a dozen large buildings. The Cancer Institute, the Heart Pavilion, the Brain and Spine Center, the Emergency Room, two professional buildings with a hundred doctors' offices. Four parking garages.

He was going to need a lot more men to do a comprehensive search of the place. He called for reinforcements to help him flush the target and his helper.

CHAPTER 11

Phoebe awoke suddenly and had a horrible couple of moments thrashing around in the dark trying to remember where she was.

"Ouch!" a groggy male voice said.

Then she remembered.

"Sorry," she said, "I didn't mean to go to sleep."

"You *snore*," Nick said.

"Are you okay?" she asked.

"I doubt it."

She sat up and tried to get her bearings. It was largely a waste of effort. The room was lit by only the faintest of light leaks from a corner of the suspended ceiling where a mouse had gnawed on it. There was no sound, no perceptible air movement.

Phoebe had no idea how long she'd been asleep. She hadn't meant to go to sleep at all, but she must've needed it. "I need to find Charlie," she said as she rubbed her face and swallowed. Her mouth tasted awful. "Wait here. I'll go see if I can find him."

He grunted a response.

She said in her most authoritative tone, "You. Stay. Here."

"Not a problem," he mumbled, from where he lay splayed out on the floor.

"I'll be back as soon as I can," Phoebe said, then she stepped into the portal, swept her magic cape around herself, and vanished.

It was surreal that two middle-aged strangers could combine forces on the spur of the moment and successfully elude half a dozen professional soldiers in a mountainous wilderness. It was like trying to catch a couple of gerbils that had gotten loose in Central Park.

Surely, the Gryphon thought, by morning it would all be over. As night approached, he watched the city go dark and the hundreds of thousands of lights come on in the buildings that ringed Central Park. It was a long time before he turned his own lights on.

The bad news about the failed hit and the unexpected escape was certain to be moving up the food chain. Heads were going to roll. He wanted to be sure his wasn't one of them.

Phoebe slid the door around on its circular track as slowly as she could, to keep any noise or visible movement to a minimum. She paused when she could peep out into the corridor. The darkroom door was set into the wall of a hallway that passed down one side of the Radiology Department.

Directly across the hall from her was an open area that held not only the abandoned wheelchair and the lead-lined protective gear, but also it contained the controls for two radiology suites, one on either side of the observation space. Counters facing each of the suites held monitors and exotic panels filled with switches and dials. The walls on both sides were made of glass so you could see into the suites.

Phoebe knew from having watched Charlie perform fluoroscopy here that each of the rooms was mostly taken up by a huge looming x-ray machine and fluoroscope that wrapped around a motorized table set on gimbals.

She looked both ways, confirmed that no one could see her, and crept across the hall into the control area. She removed a lab coat from the back of one of the rolling office chairs and put it on over her hiking clothes. Then she picked up a face shield from the counter and donned it as well to disguise herself in case anyone walked by.

Heavy-duty stainless steel prongs jutting out from the wall supported assorted bits of lead-lined protective gear—kilts, sleeveless tunics, and throat guards. She wouldn't put any of that on unless she had to because the pieces were extremely heavy.

She didn't know what time it was, but the place seemed to be empty. She thought these suites were heavily scheduled during the week, so they would be in use continuously from about 6:00 in the morning to 6:00 at night. The fact that she didn't see anyone meant it had to be late Sunday night or the wee hours of Monday morning.

She had no idea where Charlie might be. He had insomnia and preferred to work at night, but he often volunteered to fill in on weekends or for people on vacation. His home phone was unlisted, but if he was in the hospital and if she had his pager number, she could get in touch with him that way.

Even if he was at work, he could be in any of half a dozen

reading stations, as they called the darkened suites where they sat and read images on computers and dictated their findings to voice recognition. Unfortunately she had no idea how to go about finding his number and she wasn't sure how to look for him without being seen.

She didn't have a cell phone, but even if she had, she didn't know if it would work underground and in these shielded areas. She didn't see any phones except the ones on the wall that were for in-house calls only. Landlines to the outside were in each of the private offices, but she knew those were kept locked.

She crept down to where she thought Charlie's office was and found a door with his name on it. She tried the knob, but it was locked. She wracked her brain for ideas…and then she got one.

She went back to the fluoroscopy suites and went into one to take a visual inventory of the supplies. She didn't see what she was looking for, so she crossed over to the suite on the other side. She heard voices approaching, so she stepped behind a privacy curtain and stood perfectly still, holding her breath. The sounds of conversation came close and then passed by and kept going.

She stepped out from behind the curtain saw what she was looking for—a bag of a clear liquid hanging from an IV pole. She went to it and read the label, diatrizoic acid. She knew what that was. It was contrast medium, a liquid that looked clear to the human eye, but was opaque to radiation.

Some of the radiological agents went into the bloodstream, some were inhaled, and some were safe to drink. But it was obvious from the fitting on the end of this particular bag that it was intended for use on the lower end of the digestive tract. It was an enema tip.

Phoebe checked to make sure there was a cassette loaded into the holder underneath the center of the table. Then she rummaged around until she found the stash of plastic cups used to feed the patients barium.

She opened the stopcock on the bag containing the contrast medium and let about a fourth of a cup of the liquid to flow through the enema tip into the plastic cup. Then she closed the valve.

She thought about what she wanted to say, then dipped her index finger into the liquid and began to write across the top of the x-ray table.

CHAPTER 12

When Phoebe finished writing her message she wiped the dye off her finger and returned to the control area where she donned a kilt, tunic, and neck guard. Then she went into the fluoroscopy suite and positioned the cross hairs of the x-ray machine atop what she'd written and touched the *on* switch and took a single exposure. She didn't know how to calibrate the machine, so she could only hope that its automated features would set it on something that would work for her purposes.

She went back to the control area to view the image she'd made. After several seconds it began to emerge on the monitor facing the room she'd been in. It was perfectly legible. Good. Now she needed to enter some patient identification information and figure out a way to get it to a place where Charlie, and only Charlie, would see it.

She typed on the keyboard, naming the patient Zinc Phoebe Zinc, using a hybrid of her own name and the naming convention employed by the hospital to identify John Doe emergencies—people who came in without any identification, or who'd had their clothes cut off in the ambulance or helicopter, or who were in too dire a condition to wait for anyone to go through their pockets.

John Does were named in order, starting with Alpha Alpha and progressing to Zinc Zinc, at which point it started all over again with Alpha Alpha.

Phoebe put her own distinctive name in the middle to attract Charlie's attention. She knew it was possible to send the image and a message to his email, but she didn't know how to do that. So she returned to the fluoroscopy suite and removed the heavy nine-by-twelve-inch metal-edged cassette from underneath the table and carried it down the hall to Charlie's office where she left it propped against his door.

"We're lucky it's the middle of the night," she said to Nick, when she'd returned to their hiding place. There's hardly anyone around. The equipment in this area almost never gets used until the day shift."

She'd gleaned what supplies she could during her outing and shared them with Nick: pillows, blankets, a sipping cup with a bendable straw, and bottled water. She put a pillow under his head, covered him with a couple of blankets, and made him take a few sips of the water.

She set a small plastic urinal for bed-bound male patients beside Nick. "If you need to pee," she said, "go in here."

He mumbled something incomprehensible.

"Are you hurting in your head or neck?"

"Uhn nnn."

"Can you wiggle your fingers and toes?"

She touched his hands and feet to confirm that they were still in working order.

"Can you move your arms and legs?"

He could. That was good news.

"Go back to sleep," she said, "It'll help you get better. I'll watch over you and won't leave you again."

Phoebe sat beside him in the dark and stared at nothing. Her patient's breathing was deep, slow, and even. She belatedly realized that for a guy with agoraphobia, the snug, dark little hideaway she'd found was darn near perfect.

Now all they could do was wait.

Charlie worked for several hours in the small reading room next to the Emergency Room until he caught up. Then, at about 3:00 in the morning, he decided to take a break. He approached his office with a cup of coffee in one hand and his key in the other. There was an x-ray cassette propped against the door. *Residents*, he thought, *what now?*

He unlocked the door, picked up the heavy cassette, and carried it with him as he went inside. There were no notes explaining what was wanted, but that was typical. He juggled his coffee and the awkward cassette and went to the central control area. He tapped a key to wake up the screen, and logged into the special software system used by radiologists, called PACS, short for Picture Archiving and Communications System.

There was a message waiting for him. He opened it and it said, *please read the image on the cartridge immediately.*

Yeah, uh huh, sure, he thought, that image and a zillion more that awaited him.

Since the advent of CT, MRI, PET, and their even more exotic cousins, there was an endless flood of images to be read. It was a never-ending parade of human suffering. And nowadays many of them were true emergencies. Radiology had gone from being one of the most laid back departments in the hospital, to a place where surgeons stood in the doorway holding gloved hands in the air, waiting for him to tell them whether they needed to operate on someone who'd just come in on a helicopter with no pulse and no blood pressure.

Before all the new advances in imaging, radiology wasn't able to help much in some of the common critical care situations. Now it was crucial in the early decision-making process for all sorts of serious injuries and ailments. It had become an emergency medicine tool.

Charlie tried to keep in mind that although he was looking at static black and white shadows, somewhere there was a real live person who was bleeding, puking, screaming, or dying a few floors away.

He stood the x-ray cartridge on end and jammed it into the reader-scanner and waited. Then he turned to watch the monitor. He often had no idea what the images would be or what he was supposed to be looking for, and this time, yet again, he was forced to play the medical version of *what's wrong with this picture?*

From many years of experience, without being consciously aware of it, he braced himself. If this image hadn't been something unusual, it wouldn't have been delivered this way. It was then that he noticed the patient's name was given as Zinc Phoebe Zinc. *What the hell?*

The image revealed itself gradually from top to bottom as it was read by the scanner. It was definitely unique. In fact it was like nothing he'd ever seen before—and he'd seen everything.

There were no bones, no internal organs, no human parts whatsoever, just white cursive writing scrawled across a blank black field. He tilted his head to read it. It said, *Charlie Im in the old darkroom come NOW its Phoebe.*

CHAPTER 13

"I've heard of *disappearing* ink," Charlie said from the doorway, "but you've invented an *appearing* ink, at least for radiological purposes." He flipped a switch Phoebe hadn't known was there and the room was illuminated with soft red lights that were darkroom safe. He saw the man in the floor and knelt beside Nick.

"What exactly are we looking for?" Charlie said with his typical calm. This wasn't the first time Phoebe had involved him in one of her quirky cases.

"He fell out of a helicopter," she said.

Charlie looked up at her in surprise.

"Well, to be honest," she admitted, "he was *thrown* out."

"Why?"

"I'm not really sure, but I've noticed he has a way of getting on your nerves."

"Go ahead," Nick murmured, "talk like I can't hear you."

"How did he survive the fall?"

"Lucky bounce," Phoebe said.

"Why is he on the floor of my darkroom instead of in a bed in the Emergency Room?"

"Some scary people are after him. They followed us here, to finish the job I presume."

"How did you get him in here?"

"It wasn't easy."

"You somehow sneaked him in here, concocted a way to get a message to me, and then hid with him until I found you?"

Phoebe nodded. "And there's another factor. He's agoraphobic."

"That, I can fix. It's common for us to have to medicate people for MRIs. The meds for claustrophobia ought to work just as well for the reverse problem."

"Oh good."

"What are his symptoms?"

"He's sore, he can barely stand on his own, but nothing else that I know of for sure. He's been intermittently groggy and fainty, but his mind seems fine."

"It would be normal for him to be addled and in shock for a few hours after a bad fall. And the syncope could be related to his anxiety issues. But, if he's not badly injured, his condition should improve rapidly."

Nick groaned.

"Help me get him up," Charlie said.

Charlie was six-one and built like a pro football player. He held Nick without too much trouble, but Phoebe had to turn the door very slowly and tuck stray hands and feet inside as it spun away from her.

She waited her turn, then followed them out into the hallway. Mercifully, it was still empty, although she could hear sounds of people in the area.

"This was a good place to hide him," Charlie said. "It's brilliant, actually."

Phoebe retrieved the wheelchair and he lowered Nick into it. "Let's go for the full body scan," Charlie said. "It'll be quicker and I won't need to involve any of the x-ray techs."

Charlie rolled the chair to the GE LightSpeed Scanner and handed Nick a couple of pills he'd taken out of a nearby cabinet. He held a plastic cup of water and steadied Nick's head so he could take them. Then Phoebe helped him transfer their patient to the sled that would carry him in and out of the scanner.

Charlie went to a control area and flipped a bunch of switches. This was the part of radiology he called *knobology*. The radiologists and their technicians had to know how to operate all sorts of extremely complicated devices. "How many images will you take?" Phoebe asked.

"More than either of us can stand," he said, frowning. "But even with all the images in the world there are still significant limits to what we can see with this, you know."

Charlie studied the screens while Nick rode the slow-moving sled deeper into the maw of the scanner. "We can see broken bones or internal bleeding, but there could be multiple fatal soft tissue injuries that will never show up on a radiograph."

"Like what?" Phoebe asked.

"Like tears in vital organs. A hard jolt can tear our guts loose from the surrounding tissue. And that can rip a hole in an organ or tear a blood vessel. Then you die."

Phoebe nodded as she watched the images appear and morph on the computer monitors that were rotated 90° so as to stand on end. Charlie adjusted his viewing angles. He'd taught her the names of the slices in each of the three dimensions—*coronal, sagittal,* and *transverse.*

Watching him cursor up and down the body was like riding in a glass elevator through Nick's guts. Every time she watched Charlie do this she thought about the saying that beauty was only skin deep. She'd learned from hanging out in Radiology that it was just the opposite—the most extraordinary beauty began just beneath the skin.

There was nothing on earth more holy or more beautiful than the human body. A Charlie-eyed view of anatomy gave a deeply moving window onto the assurance that each of us was made in the image and likeness of God. Phoebe didn't know exactly what that meant, but seeing the images playing across the computer monitors, she believed it was true.

"He looks like he's in pretty good shape, especially considering what happened."

Charlie turned half a dozen switches off, and went to tell Nick what he'd found. He suggested that Nick and Phoebe change into scrubs to make them less noticeable and then he showed Phoebe one of the changing rooms where dozens of sets of blue and green scrubs were in neat stacks organized by size and color.

Charlie changed Nick while Phoebe changed herself. When

they were both in clean, nondescript clothes, Charlie and Phoebe rolled their patient back to the darkroom and tucked him in again.

"You realize of course that you don't know anything about this guy except that he's trouble," Charlie said.

"I know that he's *in* trouble," Phoebe corrected him.

"And he's gotten *you* in involved in whatever that is," Charlie said. "Just so you know, I've taken measures to minimize his ability to create any further difficulties for the next few hours."

Phoebe looked over at their patient. Whatever Charlie had given Nick was already taking effect. He was snoring with his mouth wide open.

CHAPTER 14

"You must be starving," Charlie said. "I'll go get some food and bring it to you. Be right back."

She heard the door scrape gently and he was gone.

He returned with a couple of bulging paper bags. He set them on the counter and methodically emptied them, revealing three bagels, half a dozen small containers of cream cheese, a couple of bananas, two individual boxes of Raisin Bran, a half pint of milk, three bottles of water, two paper bowls, and a handful of plastic knives and spoons.

He woke Nick and offered him something to eat, "No, thanks," he slurred.

"Have you urinated yet, since the fall?" Charlie asked.

Nick shook his head.

"Then we need for you to drink this," Charlie said, and held Nick's head with one hand and a bottle of water with the other. He helped Nick drink a decent amount of it. "It's important that you stay hydrated," he said, then gently lowered Nick's head to the pillow.

Charlie pulled two stools out from under the dusty counter

and he and Phoebe sat in the red twilight companionably. He was perfectly at ease, she realized. Sitting in the dark, or near darkness, with all hell breaking loose around him was normal for him.

It made her smile.

His calm companionship was a healing balm. It was already working miracles on Nick. A couple of painkillers and knowing that he wasn't obviously injured had really comforted him. He suffered from the impact with the rope platform, but the damage didn't seem to be anything beyond a sprained wrist, bruised ribs, some abrasions, and a blooming black eye. He was one lucky guy.

"So," said Charlie, "what's next?"

"I'm not sure," said Phoebe, as she gobbled some Raisin Bran and then tilted the bowl so she could drink the milk. "I haven't had time to think that far ahead. I guess I need to find somewhere more comfortable to hide him until he can figure out a longer-term solution. Can we go to your office? I need to use your phone."

Phoebe dialed her good friend and former co-worker Waneeta—a name that was pronounced like *Juanita*, but given to her by a mother who was a terrible speller. Phoebe brought her friend up to speed as quickly as possible.

Waneeta had been Phoebe's dispatcher at the rural home health care agency where they'd used to work, so she listened calmly without interrupting, then offered practical advice, saving the histrionics for later.

Neither of the women was unduly worried about Leon and Ivy because they were two of the most wilderness savvy people imaginable and they were on their home turf. Waneeta promised to check on them as soon as she hung up and relay Phoebe's update.

Phoebe told Waneeta about the new job and they discussed what to do with her patient while she went to work. Phoebe was beginning to feel that the mystery man was now safe enough and stable enough to consider what her further involvement should be, if any. She wondered if she should bail now. She thought maybe she should.

Before giving any advice on this, in typical fashion, Waneeta asked if he was good looking, if he was married, and his age. Phoebe noticed she didn't ask if he was a criminal. Waneeta's priorities were skewed very much to the romantic, which was one of the reasons she was currently on her fourth marriage. Phoebe thought Waneeta's new guy was a gonna be a keeper, though. Fourth time was a charm in this case.

In light of the time constraints they decided Phoebe should leave Nick sleeping where he was at least until the end of her first shift. Phoebe promised to get back in touch at the first opportunity and Waneeta wished her good luck.

As soon as she hung up the phone, Waneeta prayed for Phoebe's safety, then dialed Leon's number and left a message on his answering machine. Then she dialed Ivy's where he was likely to be staying if he wasn't at his own house.

After they left Charlie's office, he and Phoebe made a detour on the way back to the darkroom to pick up some medicine and supplies for Nick, then Charlie veered off unexpectedly and opened a glass door and held it open for Phoebe. It gave onto a small loading dock in a narrow dark alley. Buildings loomed on either side. There was a bench bolted down onto the small square of concrete.

Phoebe sat down and Charlie sat beside her, draping a pale blue hospital blanket around them both. He realized she was shaking, so he moved closer and put his arm around her. That helped.

He stared up at the stars as Phoebe had often seen him do when they came out of the hospital at night. Phoebe supposed it was an automatic gesture for him whenever confronted with a black field sprinkled with pale white. He was reading the night sky, just as he read radiographs.

"There's Venus," he said pointing. "And see the three stars in a row? That's Orion's belt. You can see the Pleiades, the Seven Sisters, in your peripheral vision, they're too faint tonight to be seen by looking directly at them."

Phoebe tried to do what he said and it worked. *Hmmm*, peripheral vision was more light-sensitive than direct vision. She thought about the fact that certain things were seen best by not looking at them directly. Some were too faint to be seen head on—like stars. Others were too bright—like solar eclipses. Gradually she stopped shaking.

"What do you want to do with this guy next?" Charlie asked. "The Radiology Department will start to get busy soon. He can stay in the darkroom. It's never used. In fact, most of us have forgotten about it. The young people—residents, techs, and nurses—don't even realize it's there. They wouldn't know what it was for. But if you do that, neither of you can go in or out until it gets really quiet again."

"My new job starts in a few hours," Phoebe said. "I can't stay here. I need that job, so I *have* to go. I guess I could leave him and come back tonight and get him. That'll give me time to figure out what to do with him."

Charlie nodded. "What's the job?"

"Private duty nurse. That's all I know. It's at some place in the back of beyond just over the state line in North Carolina. A ritzy-sounding English lady called to hire me."

"There are a lot of extremely wealthy people congregating over near Asheville these days. The world has discovered the Smokies. That'll be a long commute for you, though, won't it? I hope the job is something you'll enjoy."

"I like to work. And I like being a nurse. I don't even mind the cranky patients who drive everybody else crazy."

"Obviously, because you pick them up everywhere you go, like cockleburs," Charlie laughed and hugged her from the side. She lay her head over on his broad shoulder and thanked God for friends.

They sat quietly for a few more minutes, then Charlie said, "We'd better get going if you're gonna be on time for your new job."

Phoebe stood up and folded their blanket. Charlie took in her appearance and said, "I'll get you some clean scrubs and a lab coat. That way you won't have to go home and change.

Phoebe smiled her thanks.

"Let's go break the news to your patient."

CHAPTER 15

When he heard the plan to leave him in the darkroom all day, Nick panicked. "Don't leave me," he said, with more sincere emotion than she'd seen from him thus far. He grabbed her wrist in a death grip.

"I've got to go to work," Phoebe explained. "I'll come back for you tonight. I promise."

"Please," he begged, "take me with you!"

"This is my first day in a new place and with a new patient. I have no idea what the setup will be there. If I took you, you'd have to stay in the truck for eight hours until my shift is over."

"No problem."

"I can try to bring you food and water and check on you during my breaks, but you'll have to stay put. If anyone sees you, I could lose my job. And I *need* that job. Can I trust you to behave?"

"*Yes*," Nick swore emphatically.

She didn't believe him for a minute, but she felt sorry for him, so she agreed.

"If they were watching the entrances, they're undoubtedly watching the exits and maybe even the garages," Charlie said. "You can take my car. I'll go get it for you."

Phoebe loved cars more than almost anything and Charlie was offering her his Porsche Cayenne SUV. But she had a phobia about damaging other people's property, so she reluctantly turned down the generous offer.

"At least let me go get your car and bring it around for you."

Phoebe agreed to that and explained where she'd left Leon's truck. Charlie brought the wheelchair and she bundled Nick up like a real patient, which he was. Then she filled his lap with pillaged supplies, including two more pairs of scrubs. Then she covered it all with a blanket.

As Charlie rolled him down the hall, Phoebe noticed the woozy longing backwards glance Nick gave the little darkroom. She knew they'd both miss their peaceful little hidey-hole.

Charlie pushed Nick toward the same loading dock where he'd taken Phoebe earlier and told then both to wait inside until be brought Leon's truck around. He didn't go straight to the garage, but instead wound through the hospital trying to see if he was picking up a tail. He made a few stops on the way, saw nothing suspicious, then went to the parking area.

First he brought his own car out and parked it in the alley. Then he went underground to where Phoebe had left Leon's vehicle. He approached the little truck cautiously, looking for anyone who might be lurking in the area.

He didn't see anyone, but just as he pulled out of the garage and drove up onto the road that would lead him to the back of the main building, they saw each other. A black SUV with blacked out windows sat parked in a *No Parking* zone with the engine running.

Charlie took out his cell phone and made a call to hospital security. He reported a suspicious vehicle and asked them to check it out immediately. He drove away slowly until he saw a police car with flashing lights pull up and block the SUV against the curb.

When Phoebe opened the door to Leon's truck she saw that Charlie had put extra food in the passenger's footwell. He must've pillaged the Doctor's Lounge again.

"And there's a cup of hot chocolate from Starbucks in the cup holder, with extra whipped cream," he said. He knew Phoebe didn't drink coffee or alcohol.

He handed her an envelope full of cash, winked, and said, "There's an ATM in the lobby, next to the Starbucks."

"And here's a disposable cell phone. They sell these in the gift shop now. What a world! It's in my name, so nobody can use it to trace you, as far as I know. Then he told her about the SUV and the hospital security and said they needed to hurry. When Phoebe turned to Nick to see how he'd taken the news, he was asleep. She spoke to him and lightly slapped his face, but got only an incomprehensible slur in response. She looked at Charlie in panic.

He looked like a guilty, but proud, little boy.

"What did you give him?"

"Something strong. I don't trust him, and I didn't want him to jeopardize your job, or you life, so I put him down for awhile. And I gave you a few more, in case you need them later." He pointed toward the pile of stuff in the floor of the truck.

"Well thanks, I think," she said, "Now you'll have to help me get him loaded." She realized her accidental pun and looked up at Charlie to see if he'd noticed it. He had.

In his current condition, there was no way Nick could ride in the front, so Charlie helped Phoebe lay him out in the back of the pickup. They tucked a couple of blankets around him as best they could, then looked at each other, thinking the same thing. The wind would blow them off him when she reached highway speeds.

Just behind the cab there was a tangle of bungee cords and tie-downs resting in an untidy heap. They reached for them at the same time.

When they had the blankets bungeed around Nick and had him strapped and ratcheted snugly into the bed of the little truck, Charlie opened the door and held it for Phoebe. "Get in and go, and don't look back. Don't stop for *anything*."

Then he outlined his plan for getting her away from the hospital minus her tail.

Phoebe started the truck and waited for Charlie to get into his Porsche. He followed her closely as she drove toward the tiny guardhouse and gates that everyone had to pass through before leaving the hospital grounds.

Phoebe waited in line in the Visitors' lane, then paid her dollar, and the little red plank raised to let her pass. She waved at Charlie and took off for North Carolina.

When Charlie's turn came, he spoke to the lady in the booth. He knew her well. They'd both worked at the hospital for decades. He asked her for a favor and she was only too happy to grant it. Things were pretty dull on the 11-7 shift and she looked forward to a chance for some excitement.

He told her he needed her to delay the SUV that would be coming behind him. He described the color and the blacked out windows. He asked her to put up the tire shredders if necessary to make sure the vehicle didn't get out. She winked and said she'd take care of it.

She raised the gate for Charlie and he drove a short way down the exit road, pulled off to the side, and waited with his lights off.

The friendly guard did as he'd asked and after a couple of tense moments, the SUV ended up with shredded tires. It wouldn't be going anywhere. But Charlie was patient and thorough, so he continued to wait, just to be sure.

Half a minute later, a second SUV came tearing around the corner from the garage and, seeing the hoopla going on around the tire shredder, the driver swerved toward the Employees' exit lane, which was totally automated and therefore unattended. He crashed through the plank barrier and floored it.

Charlie moved around the curve of the exit road and pulled his car sideways across the narrowest section where it ran under an overpass before spiraling up onto the main road. He was totally blocking the only route to the main road. He threw his door open, leaped out, and scrambled up the steep grassy bank to make his way back to the hospital.

The second SUV came racing around the curve and the driver saw the obstruction too late. He slammed on the brakes, but still t-boned the Porsche so hard he knocked it over onto its side.

Charlie was smart. Nobody would be giving chase for a good long while. She'd be able to get away safely now. He glanced up at the stars again before going back inside, then he returned to his office and called his insurance agent.

CHAPTER 16

Blissfully unaware of Charlie's automotive sacrifice, Phoebe sped away through the night. She looked in the rear view mirror every few minutes to make sure Nick was still back there and still sleeping soundly.

Dawn had broken by the time she made it to the crest of the Great Smoky Mountains. This was the boundary between Tennessee and North Carolina. The highest part of the Appalachian Trail ran along this same ridge on a trail that was so narrow a hiker's left foot would be in one state and their right foot in another.

It had been such a shock when the call about the new job came, Phoebe had transcribed the directions without really taking them in. Since then she'd been busy. She hadn't really had the opportunity to think much about where she was headed, or consider the route she'd be taking to get there.

The novelty hit her when she turned onto the six-mile long *Road to Nowhere,* as it was referred to by the locals. In the directions, Ms. Arabella Devlin-Forrest had referred to it by a state road number that Phoebe hadn't recognized. Now she knew why. She'd never been there before. Why would she have been? The road was a famous dead end.

Now that she realized where she was, she recalled that the

original plan for the road was that it would skirt the edge of Fontana Lake and give people on the North Carolina side of the mountain access to family graveyards that were inside the boundaries claimed by the National Park in the 1930's.

The Great Smoky Mountains National Park differed from the other major national parks in two significant ways. First, it was the most popular park in the nation by a long shot. It got two to three times as many visitors as the Grand Canyon or Yellowstone or Yosemite. And second, it had been created on private property by ejecting the local families from their homes.

Hard feelings still abounded. People were forced out and watched helplessly as their homes were bulldozed or allowed to fall into ruin, and access to family graveyards was restricted. It wasn't like this was ancient history either. Plenty of people were still alive who'd been born and raised on beautiful mountain farms that the U.S. government had taken from them by force.

But the cost of building a road across such a remote mountainous wilderness for access to the North Carolina graveyards was incredibly expensive and had gradually been halted. That meant people had to travel across Fontana Lake by boat to reach them on Decoration Day.

Phoebe knew the *Road to Nowhere* ended in a quarter-mile long oddity called the *Tunnel to Nowhere*. When she read the portion of the directions that concerned the tunnel, Phoebe thought, *how could that be right?* The incredibly expensive tunnel had been completed just before the road construction was abandoned, and as far as Phoebe knew, there was no road on the other side of it. Thus, its nickname.

The mountains in this area made cell phone service extremely spotty, to say the least. So before she lost all possibility of contact with civilization Phoebe stopped and called Waneeta again to let her know she was alright. Then she asked for news from the café.

"They's no new bodies showed up, if that's what you mean," Waneeta said. "Leon and Ivy are fine and they said to tell you they brought your Jeep back and hid it in Leon's barn. The key's in it, if you need it."

Phoebe gave Wanteeta, and thereby the entire community of White Oak, an update on her activities, her patient, and her near term plans. She knew her escapades would provide much good-natured entertainment for her friends and neighbors.

She hung up, relieved of her worries about her friends. She needed to be able to concentrate if she was going to successfully navigate this mysterious segment of her commute. The directions made no sense. She read them aloud to herself, *Turn right after passing through the tunnel.*

The tunnel was a well-known landmark to hikers, but no one ever drove into it because it was dark, spooky, and a dead-end. At least it was supposed to be. Phoebe sat facing the black hole with her high beams illuminating the curved mossy ceiling and walls. She couldn't see any obstacles but neither could she see any light in the distance. That was ominous, but she gamely began to move into the darkness, rolling slowly along the pavement. There were leaves scattered on the ground, but otherwise the surface was in surprisingly good condition.

Phoebe crept along in Leon's ancient little truck, farther and farther into the gloom until she knew she had to be nearing the end of the tunnel. Then she stopped when her headlights illuminated what appeared to be a solid wall of moss-covered concrete in front of her. A moment later she felt something give underneath her.

She opened the driver's side door and looked down. She could see that she was sitting on a segment of pavement that was about twenty feet long and separated from the rest of the road by a thin crack at both ends. It was like a truck scale, but concealed.

There was a low grinding noise and the wall in front of her started to move. A second later, there was light at the end of the tunnel.

Abracadabra, she whispered, in awed tones. She couldn't think of anything else to say. The magnitude of this deception stunned her. The level of power, privacy, and security represented by a secret entrance like this was beyond anything she'd ever heard of.

The world was being turned on its head, *again*, for the second time in two days. What the heck was going on? And what had she done to be drawn into the vortex?

Phoebe had no idea who she was on her way to see. It wasn't unusual for a rural home health care nurse to be dispatched to care for a stranger. The nurses went wherever they were called. Phoebe's previous work had covered a large, highly dispersed, rural community. But it was odd to not have been given the patient's name. She'd been so happy to get a job, it hadn't occurred to her to question it. She'd blithely assumed she was going to see an eccentric musician, but now she doubted if that was sufficient to explain the tunnel gambit unless it was Elvis.

She came out into bright sunshine on the other side of the high ridge. She rolled carefully along the last remaining bit of paved road that became a manicured pea gravel lane that led up a slight hill. When she topped the rise she was presented with a glorious view. A vast, endless hardwood forest stretched before her, covering the undulations of countless green ridges that, in the distance, disappeared into the world famous blue haze.

Trees and sky as far as the eye could see. Nothing made by

the hand of man disrupted the landscape. That was an increasingly unusual phenomenon these days. Unspoiled panoramas were already nearly nonexistent on the Tennessee side, and now were becoming rare on the North Carolina side, which had historically been protected from overdevelopment by having far fewer roads through the areas adjacent to the Park.

Two miles to the house, said her scribbled notes. Phoebe continued until the road came to another apparent dead end. She sat in the little truck, not moving. She was facing a pile of boulders at point blank range. They were poised on the edge of a bluff with a tumble of fractured rock typical of the area. Beyond the boulders, the ground fell away for hundreds of feet in a sheer rock face.

She opened her door and got out.

CHAPTER 17

Phoebe stood quietly next to the truck, looking around, enjoying the soft breeze and the splendid view. Then she checked Nick. His breathing and pulse were excellent. His skin was a nice healthy pink except for the left side of his face where he was developing a colorful black eye. He seemed to be recovering nicely. She knew this deep, drugged-induced sleep would be healing for him after all the stress he'd experienced.

She thought about untying him, but remembered how her ranger friend Henry always held wild critters down until he was certain they were wide awake so they couldn't accidentally wander into a road or a river or fall off a cliff on account of being woozy.

With a cliff this close, Phoebe didn't dare untie Nick. She tugged a corner of one of the blankets loose, though, and rearranged it, draping it over a tie-down so it would keep the sun off his face.

She walked toward the edge of the cliff, along the row of boulders, and called out, "Hello!"

When no one responded, she took a few paces toward a particularly large rock, and then went around the side of it. There was a large natural crevice between two of the massive stones that was wide enough to walk through.

When she stepped through the gap she found herself in an open area filled with immaculately maintained gardens. On the other side of the garden was a house, or at least what she presumed was a house. It was built right into the jagged rocks at the edge of the cliff.

As she made her way along a neat path through the garden toward what looked like it might be the front door, she noticed the landscaping was mostly edible. It was vegetables mixed with herbs and flowers, but it was so artfully done, it was even more appealing to Phoebe, who'd been raised on a farm, than a purely decorative grouping of non-native flowers planted for curb appeal.

The stacked stone and boulder walls that enclosed the garden were faced with trellises that supported espaliered fruit trees, vines, and various types of running and climbing plants. Near the front door was a large expanse of vertical garden mounted on a metal grid. Phoebe smiled to see several varieties of salad greens sprouting at eye level.

A row of beehives stood along one side of the garden. The stacks of wooden boxes were painted in a charming hodgepodge of pale blues and pinks. Each hive had a name painted in large ornate letters on the topmost box—Uriel, Raphael, Gabriel, Samael, and Oriphiel.

There was a large ornate metal knocker in the shape of a winged angel mounted on an ancient-looking gothic-shaped wooden door. Phoebe used it to tap twice and then she waited. After a couple of minutes a woman near her own age opened the door and said, "Ms. McFarland, I am Arabella Devlin-Forrest, please forgive me for not meeting you outside and escorting you in, but I was engaged on a telephone call."

The woman wore an immaculate coatdress that looked like one of designs Catherine Walker made especially for the royal family.

And she spoke with the same upper class English accent Phoebe remembered hearing on the phone. "If you will come this way, please. I will take you to your patient."

Phoebe reminded herself to do her best to speak Standard English to these people. They obviously were not local. She followed Arabella down a short flight of wide shallow stone stairs into the house, expecting to enter a cave-like space, but it was quite the opposite. The far wall of the house was all glass, giving a view across the mountains like something she thought eagles might have. The floor was concrete that had been ground and polished until it shone like a mirror. It was reflecting the light from skylights, creating a mirage so that the large expanse stretching out before them was shimmering like the surface of a lake.

The house was built atop, within, and around boulders—and the natural rock had been left exposed. As they walked, Phoebe saw that the house was lit not only by skylights and a glass wall, but also occasionally from the side by windows with eccentric shapes made to fit the natural crevices.

She stole quick glances into the rooms they passed as Arabella escorted her through the house. A small creek ran through the center of what looked like a living area, and she heard and then saw a natural waterfall at the far end of a hall.

The house was quiet except for the sound of water. It had a soothing effect on her frazzled nerves.

CHAPTER 18

"I don't know my patient's name," Phoebe said.

Arabella hesitated a moment and then said, "You may address him as *Le Seigneur.*" She pronounced his title in French to sound like *sane-yeur.*

"Like *senior?*" Phoebe asked.

"If you are enquiring about the etymology of the word, yes, the roots are the same. If you are enquiring about the modern meaning, *Le Seigneur* is a French honorific that means *Lord.*"

"*Lord?*" Phoebe repeated, flabbergasted. She couldn't help herself but her first thought was, *Oh Lord, what have I gotten myself into?* Fortunately she was able to keep her reflexive outburst to herself.

The people of the Smoky Mountains were possibly the least hierarchical ethnic group on the face of the earth. Respect had to be earned. Their natural hyper-politeness and tendency to be amused would instantly leap to its polar opposite, insolence, when presented with anyone they deemed to be affecting airs.

"I don't think I can call him that with a straight face," Phoebe said.

She followed Arabella into the room and saw an elderly man

lying in bed. He'd obviously heard their exchange because he gave her a gentle smile and said, "My name is Étienne."

Phoebe smiled back at him, and tilted her head to try to work out what he'd said. Whatever he'd said, it was pronounced with a honking sound she'd have to work on.

"In English it is rendered as *Steve*." He spoke with a strong French accent.

Phoebe looked at the room and at her patient and decided it wouldn't be right to call him Steve. Her patient's room was light, and airy, but as stark as a monk's cell. It contained a bed, a nightstand, and a single chair, all made of scrubbed pine that glowed with the warm golden patina of beeswax polish and age.

She guessed the man was in his seventies. "Please have a seat," he said. "Thank you so much for coming."

Books and papers lay all around him atop the covers.

"I'm still adjusting to the new technology," he said, flourishing a pencil in his right hand. "I am learning to dictate to voice recognition. It works almost perfectly, but I find myself unable to compose text unless I'm holding a pencil."

They both laughed.

"I hope it wasn't too difficult finding us." He had an angelic smile.

Phoebe shook her head, deciding not to make any comment on the extraordinary features of his driveway. She was suddenly too shy to meet his dark-eyed gaze, so she cast her eyes around the room.

The only decoration was an exquisite miniature that sat on a small easel atop his bedside table. It was a painting of a knight in armor facing a dragon. Phoebe guessed it must be either St. George or St. Michael, but she didn't know how to tell the difference. It depicted a charming scene where the two opposing figures seemed to be having a chat rather than a battle.

"That's lovely," Phoebe said. "I've never seen one like that. The knight and the dragon seem to be friends."

"There's no point at being angry at the Devil," he said. "The Devil is only doing his job." He gave her another sweet smile, then added, "But, of course it's our responsibility to see him for what he is and not join in on the wrong side of things."

"Is this St. Michael or St. George?"

"It is St. Michael, the archangel. He is the greatest spiritual being of his rank, the chief of the angels and the archangels. I am glad you notice the tone of the image. Only the relatively newer versions depict any aggression between the angel and the dragon. The oldest pictures show Michael not even looking at the dragon. He stands with his face raised to heaven, averting his eyes from the distractions of evil.

"It is like the famous quote that no problem can ever be solved with thinking that occurs on the same level where the problem was created. Problems can only be solved with higher thinking. In the Bible, in Jude, the Archangel Michael speaks to the Devil, but he is careful in how he does it. He says, *The Lord rebuke thee*. He says this because it is not man's task to rebuke the devil, but God's.

"St. George comes on the scene much later. He is the one you almost always see fighting. That's because he is a man rather than an angel. He is a human trying to overcome evil. This task is more difficult, more confusing, for a human than it is for an angel. Angels don't have free will."

Phoebe saw that her patient's face was creased and lined.

Careworn or disease-worn, she didn't yet know. She might've been wrong about her initial guess at his age. Now that she was closer, and as the clouds shifted overhead so the light coming in through the skylight changed and played across his face, something about his face made her think he might just as easily be much older.

Phoebe was going to ask him about his condition and what she could do for him, but before she could speak, a beautiful young woman appeared in the doorway wearing a white cotton nun's habit with blue stripes along the border, like the one Mother Teresa had worn. She didn't say anything but she and *Le Seigneur* exchanged a look of concern.

He turned to Phoebe and said, "We would like to bring your friend inside, if you do not mind."

Phoebe was shocked and embarrassed that they'd managed to discover Nick, and so quickly, too. "I'm *so sorry*," she said, mortified. "I know this is highly irregular, but it was an emergency. I hope you'll forgive me for bringing somebody along, especially on my first day, but there was nowhere else for him to go."

"Please do not worry," he said. "Tell me about him."

Phoebe gave her patient a highly sanitized and extremely brief version of Nick's backstory. She said she'd found him after he'd had a bad fall in the forest and he didn't have any insurance. *Le Seigneur* listened attentively, with emotions playing across his expressive face.

When Phoebe finished, he said, "I understand," and made a quick nod toward the nun. He indicated with a graceful gesture that Phoebe should go with her.

Just before they went out the front door, Phoebe laid a hand on the nun's arm and said, "You'd better let me go get him by myself. He's been through a lot recently and he might be frightened by a stranger."

The nun made a small bow and remained in the foyer while Phoebe went outside. When she cleared the boulders and crunched across the pea gravel toward the truck, she saw that the mummy was getting restless. He was kicking against his shroud.

Phoebe leaned over the bed of the truck and released the tie-downs. Nick was still wrapped in the soft blue hospital blankets that were bungeed around him in three different places. It was a struggle not to laugh at his appearance, but Phoebe was a pro, so she maintained a poker face.

Nick sat up and gave her a dirty look. "Are we there yet?" he asked, sarcastically.

CHAPTER 19

Phoebe unhooked the bungee cords and unwrapped the blankets. Then she helped Nick climb out of the back of the truck. He was surprisingly bright and alert. She told him that he'd been invited inside. "Be good," she warned.

Nick kept his mouth shut as he was met by the young nun and escorted through the extraordinary house. She led them to what was obviously a kitchen. It was a marvel of bronze sinks, copper pots, wooden spoons, and exposed pipes in a style that was a collision between the Flintstones and some very rich tree-huggers. "*Le Seigneur* suggests you refresh yourselves," she said, gave them a small bow, and left.

A young man stood at a counter across the room with his back to them. He was chopping vegetables on a cutting board made from a slice of a tree that still had bark around the edges. The counter he worked on was an immense slab of honed soapstone.

This was not just rich, thought Phoebe, but a special kind of bottomless pit of wealth. A beautiful house like this, hidden in plain sight, was several levels beyond the best security system money could buy. She could tell Nick was awestruck, too.

The monk-chef was dressed in a perfectly clean, hand-woven brown medieval-style monk's robe that was belted with a real rope.

"Allow me make you breakfast," he said, with a thick Scottish accent. "What would you like? We have a full range of seasonal organic produce grown locally. Breads. Free range eggs, goat or cow's milk. Cheeses.

"What do you recommend?" asked Phoebe, utterly charmed.

"The goat cheese omelet is very popular, but I prefer the slow food version of the Egg McMuffin."

Phoebe laughed and ordered the healthy McMuffin. Nick went for the goat cheese omelet. The two shell-shocked houseguests sat side-by-side on stools at a vast limestone island wolfing down the delicious meal. Nick was clearly feeling better by the minute.

Phoebe figured now was as good a time as any to try to find out exactly what she'd gotten herself into by befriending him. She didn't want to take him into the room with her new boss totally unprepared.

"We haven't had much of an opportunity to get to know each other. But, considering the circumstances, I need to cut right to the chase. Why are people trying to harm you?" she asked, putting it as gently as she could.

Nick shrugged, "The guys weren't much for conversation, but I gleaned that they'd prefer that I not publish the results of my research."

"What research would that be?"

"I'm writing a book about the actual cause of the Civil War."

Phoebe was dumbfounded. Talk about anti-climactic.

"Instead of debating with me about my methodology in obscure economics and history journals," he said, "they decided it would be more expedient to simply toss me out of a helicopter in a place where no one would ever find my body."

Wow. That seemed a like an extremely disproportionate reaction to a boring problem. She turned sideways to look at him. He didn't seem to be kidding. As usual, when confused, Phoebe reverted to dialect. "What're you sayin? That there's still people fightin the Civil War? Like those reenactor people?"

Nick shook his head, so Phoebe continued with her list of suspects, "The Daughters of the Confederacy? The Ku Klux Klan?"

"No and no," Nick said. "My guess is that it's one or more large corporations."

Oh my gosh, Phoebe thought, *he's insane.*

Nick saw the look on her face. "I know it sounds paranoid, but I'm a mathematician. I've done the regression analyses over and over and I've run it by the best economists in the country, even Nobel Prize winning economists, and everyone agrees that I'm correct."

"About *what?*" Phoebe asked.

"That slavery was not the cause of the American Civil War."

Uh oh, Phoebe thought, now she had an inkling why people were trying to kill Nick. This kind of talk was certain to send knee-jerk left-wingers and the political correctness police into orbit. Apparently it already had.

The cause of the Civil War was supposed to be black and white, north and south, good and evil, plain and simple. It looked like she'd accidentally gotten hooked up with a Salman Rushdie type. A political correctness fatwa must've been put out on him.

"Abolition was a smokescreen concocted by northern industrialists who stood to make fortunes if they could block imports from England that were undercutting their sales. Before the Civil War and during the generations since then, robber barons have spent a lot of money obfuscating the fact that there is a direct correlation between tariffs—taxes on imports—and war."

Phoebe tried to choose her words carefully. "I know this is somethin that's real important to you, and I don't wanna upset you, but what you just said is a totally toxic mixture of extremely boring and yet unbelievably inflammatory stuff."

"Exactly! If you link a despicable human rights practice to a dull business matter, everyone will tune you out. And yet, imposing certain types of tariffs on particular types of imports is how you start wars all over the world. And I have proof."

Nick was certainly animated all of a sudden. This was a new side of his character she'd not seen before.

"Many industries in addition to the so-called military-industrial complex, want to prevent this information from getting out. They will gleefully kill me to prevent the public from finding out how they light these fuses around the world and then reap vast profits from behind the screen of their war-mongering."

Phoebe struggled to follow what he was saying.

"It's been going on for centuries. One of the lies is that the only companies that profit from wars are the ones that make weapons or military provisions. The truth is that even greater fortunes are being made in ostensibly unrelated industries. It's *these* guys who're the ones actually starting the wars—like the textile trades started the Civil War—and the automotive industry, among others, is fomenting conflict in modern times."

"Why hasn't anyone noticed this?" Phoebe asked, still not sure he wasn't nuts.

"The root cause of the conflict is subtle. You can't explain the concept in a sound bite, and it doesn't help that winners of wars always rewrite history and cover up the incriminating parts. But also, we're a nation where voting your pocketbook without the slightest concern for your fellow men or for the future of civilization has become *the way things are done.*"

Phoebe didn't say anything. She wanted to care, but she just didn't. She was a nurse, he was a numbers guy. She was more interested in his black eye than World War III.

"He's right, of course," said the monk-chef, from across the room. He was stirring a stockpot of soup with his back to them. "There are various sorts of groups—you can label them interest groups, trade associations, political parties, call them what you like.

"The front men for these cabals are never the real leaders. They're just puppets who fit a vital demographic. They're good looking, eloquent. They're recruited and groomed for their roles.

"The top people are never publicly revealed, and they're rarely known, even to the most ardent and highly-placed followers. These groups have legions of enforcers. It sounds like you've had a run-in with them."

He put a lid on the pot and turned to collect their plates. "Good people, honest people, can't afford to be naïve and trusting, *or disinterested,*" he said, looking pointedly at Phoebe. "That's how evil wins."

He removed a tin of glorious smelling apple and cinnamon muffins from the oven and set it down in front of them. He waggled his oven mitts at them and added, "But if you're going to engage with these rascals, you better have the proper protection."

CHAPTER 20

After they'd both scarfed a warm muffin, the monk-chef said, "Arjun will take you to *Le Seigneur*."

Nick visibly flinched when he looked over his shoulder and saw the tall, fierce-looking fellow standing nearby wearing Sikh garb—a large turban in a brilliantly-hued orange and a white robe over loose white pants. Arjun delivered them to their destination in silence. A second chair had appeared in his room during Phoebe's absence.

"Come," he said. "It is a pleasure to have you both here. Quite enlivening, I must say. It can be annoying to have opposition, but it is strengthening as well. Like exercise, it is the way of things here on Earth, is it not?"

Phoebe and Nick both nodded, too befuddled to speak. There was something about the man that radiated great wisdom and kindness. He was obviously very frail. There were countless tiny lines radiating from around his eyes and mouth. But his large, expressive dark brown eyes had not been touched by age. They were beautiful.

"You are safe here," he said, looking at Nick.

For reasons she would have been hard pressed to articulate, Phoebe relaxed for the first time since she'd met Nick, and when she did, she realized how sore she was from all the unaccustomed sorts of activity and the terrible tension.

"What *is* this place?" Nick asked.

Le Seigneur considered the question. "You might surmise it is a monastery because of the students who come here to study and work, but the days for cloisters are over. No more cowering, or lazing, behind high walls. We must do our work out in the world. *In* the world, but not *of* the world, of course."

Nick nodded.

"To be perfectly accurate one should refer to this place as a *School for Mysteries*," *Le Seigneur* said.

"Mysteries?" Phoebe echoed, "A School for Mysteries?" She had no idea what he meant.

"*Magnum Mysterium.* There are those of us who have made it our life's task to investigate the Great Mystery—God and man, the meaning of life, what happens after we die, those sorts of questions."

Phoebe was extremely confused now, sandwiched between the mystery of Nick and the mystery of her new boss.

"The Mystery Schools of antiquity were conducted in the strictest secrecy. Only recently has it become permissible to work openly. There are many who oppose this lack of secrecy—especially the dark brotherhoods. But we cannot allow ourselves to be deterred by the dark ones. So, here we are, esoteric, what some might call *mystical,* religious scholars and translators of all stripes, working to answer the big questions.

"You allow males and females to study together?" Phoebe asked, surprised.

"Of course. All the *real* Mystery Schools have always allowed this, encouraged it, even *required* it. We are sent to earth in two genders for a reason. We must bring both skill sets to all the important questions. It is absurd, it is *evil,* to do otherwise."

Phoebe was starting to really like her new boss.

"Another feature that identifies a real Mystery School is the working together of mixed faiths, such as Moslems, Christians, and Jews. The mystical branches of all the major world religions agree about the important spiritual truths."

Le Seigneur studied their faces. "Here you will find the current embodiment of a line that goes back thousands of years. Rama, Krishna, Hermes, Moses, Orpheus, Pythagoras, Plato, Jesus. There is quite a bit to know, if you are interested.

"But, of course, that is for another day. For now we have more pressing matters to attend to. I must say, it is very diverting to have the opportunity to intersperse the big questions with the occasional smaller mystery, a *parvus mysterium,* like yours."

Le Seigneur looked at Nick and said, "You, we knew of." Then he looked back at Phoebe and said, "You, we did not know of, until now." He smiled his lovely smile, and said, "Tell me how you really met."

Phoebe gave him a slightly revised and expanded description of the events of the previous two days. He clapped his hands with glee, looked at Nick, and said, "Cast out of heaven and fallen to earth to make your way down here amongst the rest of us poor rabble. Painful and frightening for you certainly, but what wonderful image. What an entrance!"

He laughed, which made him look much younger, and added, "Cosmic humor at it's best."

Nick seemed unable to speak.

"*Fear not*, as they admonish us so often in the Bible," he said to Nick. "You have done a magnificent job so far and now we will help you get your work out into the world. I cannot promise they will not eventually succeed in killing you, but I can assure you that now at least you will not have died for nothing."

Ouch. That was a smack upside the head. Phoebe reached for Nick's hand. It was ice cold.

"We are always much closer to death than we realize. Our existence here is quite precarious. Especially for people like you. Light always calls to Darkness. One of the greatest mysteries of life here on earth is that wherever there is light, there is also shadow. You have reached the critical point in your destiny at which you must step out into the light. And, of course, there will be significant consequences when you do."

Nick visibly sagged.

"Buck up my friend, the great mysteries are not for sissies. Achieving ones destiny requires courage," he admonished. "Our Lord Jesus Christ demonstrated this at considerable expense for our eternal edification."

Nick nodded. Tears seeped slowly out of one eye.

"Simply staying alive can become quite a challenge at times. We each must find something we value enough to make all the pain and frustration of this place seem worthwhile. It is no good straining at life if we do not have something we love, something we can help with, something that gives all the struggle of this place meaning. And even then, sometimes we can become tired."

Le Seigneur leaned over and patted Nick on the knee, "You are not alone any more, my son. You have found your helpers now."

CHAPTER 21

"I would like to ask a favor of you," *Le Seigneur* said to Phoebe. "Would you mind escorting Nicolas to our media people? You've done a superb job with him so far. I am confident that he will remain safe in your care. The facility is less than a hundred miles from here."

"Media?" Nick asked, nearly as terrified at the idea of being interviewed in front of television cameras as he was of being caught by whoever was chasing him.

"The only solution to your problem is to get the fruits of your research out to the world. We have friends who can do that for you. You will be quite satisfied with their results, I assure you. Families who own castles are generally extraordinarily savvy about media."

Nick and Phoebe both wondered what he meant by that, but didn't have the courage to ask any more questions because they were afraid of what the answers might be.

"I have no doubt that the formidable Ms. McFarland will ensure your safe arrival."

"Of course," Phoebe heard herself say, although she didn't want to do it. This job was turning out to be a lot harder than she'd expected.

"Please allow me to provide you with fresh clothing," *Le Seigneur* said, gesturing that they should accompany Arabella.

Phoebe saw Nick flinch at the wardrobe possibilities, but she agreed and thanked her boss before Nick could make any wisecracks.

"May I suggest you avail yourselves of our bathing facilities, as well," said Ms. Devlin-Forrest, in a tone that allowed for no refusal.

A Sufi named Hakim brought them fresh clothes. He looked to be in his mid-thirties. He was wearing the dervish attire of flaring cream-colored robe with cream-colored leggings, a terracotta-colored hat that looked like an inverted flowerpot, and a red sash.

Nick wasn't exactly comfortable in the thin scrubs he'd been given by Charlie but he was also reluctant to give them up. He dreaded having to wear a turban or some other attention-getting headgear. He didn't think he could pull off a look like that, even under threat of imminent death.

He was relieved to see that the pile of neatly folded clothes given to him consisted of Calvin Klein undergarments still in their plastic wrappings, jeans in the correct size, an expensive looking black cashmere turtleneck, and a pair of very stylish black tennis shoes.

The stack of clothing for Phoebe included black leggings, a luscious charcoal gray cashmere tunic, and a pair of black Chanel ballet flats. A hot shower improved Phoebe's outlook tremendously. Another muffin and a large glass of milk made her feel ready to take on the world.

Nick was looking a lot better, too, even with his Technicolor black eye. The shiner hadn't been as obvious in the first few hours, but now it was remarkable with splotches of purple, blue, green, and yellow.

The clothing they'd been given fit both of them perfectly. It was the best either of them had looked in years.

Before they left, Nick and Phoebe returned to *Le Seigneur*'s room and stood beside his bed. "These catastrophic events that upend our lives are not random," the old man said. "Quite the opposite. The very events we tend to dismiss as *accident* or *coincidence* are in fact the most crucial meetings with our destiny that will bring us into contact with the companions necessary in order for us to perform our most significant life tasks."

He waved them closer. He took their right hands and said some words over them in a language Phoebe didn't recognize. "Please bend down," he said, then he rested his palms on the tops of their heads in blessing.

Phoebe could feel great warmth, even heat, from his hand. Then he took a deep breath and let them go, giving them a last sweet smile before lying back on his pillows, looking exhausted.

"Don't worry," he said to Phoebe, "you may come back tomorrow morning and resume your nursing duties. This afternoon, however, Nicolas' predicament must take priority."

It would take a few hours, but later Phoebe would wonder at *Le Seigneur*'s use of the word *may*. Had he been giving her permission to return, or a warning that she might not live to return?

"Ms. Devlin-Forrest will give you directions to our Media Division."

Arabella escorted them to her office. She handed Nick a hand-drawn map and a sheet of paper with directions neatly typed on it. She handed Phoebe a nylon travel wallet on a long lanyard and told here there was a cell phone inside that she should use instead of her own.

"If you encounter any difficulties with the Media Division," Arabella told her, mention the name *Archangel* and that will smooth your path."

CHAPTER 22

Nick sat in the passenger seat of Leon's little truck and scanned the map he'd been given by Arabella. Phoebe got in on the driver's side. She gave a last glance toward the innocent looking boulders that utterly camouflaged the house, looked out over the spectacular view, and then turned the little truck around and headed down the pea gravel road.

Phoebe tried not to think at all as she backtracked until they reached the concealed entrance to the *Tunnel to Nowhere*. "Check this out," she said.

Nick was suitably astonished by the mechanism that allowed them to enter. When they emerged from the public end of the tunnel Nick read out the directions that guided them farther across the mountains, deeper into North Carolina, on a route that was so complicated Phoebe doubted she'd be able to remember it.

They spoke very little. They were both simply overwhelmed. Any conversation about *Le Seigneur* and the wacky *School for Mysteries* would be totally speculative and too bizarre to for either of them to stand at this point. After a couple of hours they caught sight a city in the distance. Phoebe guessed they might be somewhere near Asheville. But she was so thoroughly discombobulated by recent events, she wouldn't have been surprised to learn it was Santa Fe.

It didn't matter anyway because they weren't going into the town. The route marked on the map indicated a turn onto an unmarked dirt track that, once it was out of sight of the road, became a well-maintained one-lane road through a dense woods.

After several miles, the lush vegetation gave way to a more manicured forest, and finally to a woodland that gave the impression of being staged. It was so picturesque, it looked as if each tree had been carefully chosen and placed to its best advantage.

Phoebe got a creeping sense of where they might be headed mere seconds before they topped a small rise, and she could see their destination. Her guess had been correct. Chateau St. Cloud was unmistakable—a full-size faux Renaissance French castle built in the early 1900s. The house was so large and opulent that its construction had seriously drained the wallet of one of the richest men in the world.

It was a regional attraction that Phoebe had visited a couple of times, once as a child and then again as a teenager. Neither time had she'd noticed that there was an access road that approached from the back. It was just one more revelation that led her to realize that there were indeed worlds within worlds and that when she'd woken up yesterday morning, she'd innocently stepped out of one and into another. Surprise!

They followed the road until it dead-ended into the base of the imposing stone wall at the back of the house. The house was what you might call a split level, except it was built on such a grand scale that the ground level on the back of the house was at least fifty feet lower than the front. The front rose at least four stories above the main entrance. So the tallest peaks in the flamboyant roof loomed well over a hundred feet above where they sat in their extremely humble, forty-year old, smoking, Datsun sub-compact pick-up truck.

Approaching a massive, sheer, blank stone wall was less worrisome now than it would've been had Phoebe not already experienced the light at the end of the infamous *Tunnel to Nowhere* and the fabulous house hidden amongst the boulders. So, Phoebe sat passively at the end of the track and waited.

"What the hell are we supposed to do now?" Nick asked.

Phoebe said nothing, then after only a few seconds, a huge door opened. It was made of perhaps ten of the gigantic stones that made up the wall. The opening was irregularly shaped to reflect the joints between the rocks. A man in the costume of an early nineteenth century chauffeur waved them inside.

"Different theme, "Nick said, "but still with the costumes."

Phoebe had to laugh. "All the people who work in the house are dressed up in costumes. The whole place is a historical reenactment."

"It's a castle! Shouldn't they be mincing around in doublets and hose, with swords?"

"That would make sense, but no, they're dressed to reflect the time the house was built, in the Gilded Age. The Titanic niche generates a lot more revenue these days than the French Renaissance."

"I can't take much more of this," Nick said. "It's all so crazy, it's eclipsing my previous neuroses."

"Yesterday was hard on both of us," Phoebe said, "the helicopter, the hospital. And today, it's not even noon and we've already had a secret tunnel, my new job started, a coed nondenominational monastery for mysteries, and now a time-travelling chateau on the wrong continent."

Nick snorted.

"We hardly know each other but, trust me, this hasn't been my typical week either," she said. "We're both doing the best we can. That's all anybody can do."

He sighed and got out of the truck. The chauffeur clicked his heels, bowed, and valet parked the vehicle with as much formality as if it had been a Rolls Royce. In fact he parked it next to a row of half a dozen of them. It looked like a timeline of Rolls Royces, from one that looked brand new, to a slightly older one, then a vintage one, and finally to an antique that had an open-top compartment over the chauffeur that exposed him to the weather while his precious passengers would remain dry.

They turned to see a young man coming toward them from the dark recesses of the cavernous garage. He looked like a tourist. He was wearing cargo pants and a t-shirt that said, *More Caffeine Please.*

"Ms. McFarland, Mr. ... ?"

"Nick. Just call me Nick."

Phoebe stepped forward and said, "Hello, I'm Phoebe. We were told to come here, but I'm afraid we're pretty confused about what happens next. It's been ... hectic."

"Understatement of the year," murmured Nick.

"No prob. Stuff happens," he said. "I'm Xander, but you can call me X. If you'll come with me, we've got a team set up and they're waiting for you in the conference room."

They had a team set up and waiting? *Okay.*

X took them to an elevator and they were whisked upwards. The doors opened onto a hall with curved walls that came to together in a point at the top, like a gothic arch. They must be in the attic, Phoebe thought, right up under the peak of the roof.

The hall itself was dimly lit but there were bright slashes of light coming in from the sides at regular intervals through dormer windows in each room they passed, most of which had the doors left wide open to share the light and the view. Phoebe tried to catch a glance through any of them to help orient her as to where they were, but she could see only sky. Apparently they were *very* high.

They continued down the hall until Xander said, "Here we go."

This time he opened a door into a room furnished like a comfortable club, complete with leather sofas, easy chairs, and a huge fireplace. The room was double-height and had a mezzanine level with a fabulously ornamented railing that around three sides. The balcony was reachable by way of a metal spiral staircase.

Three young people were already there, engaged in rapid conversation. They were holding either gigantic phones or teeny tablets. Phoebe wasn't sure which.

One of them was getting a hot drink from an extraordinary machine that looked like something out of a steampunk Starbucks. "Would either of you like something?" he asked. Nick asked for a black coffee. Phoebe wanted a hot chocolate.

Phoebe casually moved closer to a window and peered out, still trying to discern where exactly they were in relation to the vast and eccentric design of the chateau. She could tell that the room jutted out from the main structure and was four or maybe five stories off the ground. She suspected it was in the top of the central spire, perhaps above the main entrance.

Although there was no door giving access to it, there was a

narrow balcony around the outside of the room with an intricately carved stone balustrade. She wondered why anyone would want to be out there. Was it just part of the French Renaissance decoration or was it some sort of medieval fire escape?

She leaned closer to the glass and looked down. People were coming and going directly below her. They looked very small from this distance. She felt herself getting dizzy and turned around to face into the room. Phoebe hated heights.

X introduced them to the half a dozen young people now assembled and said they were an emergency referral from the *Archangel*. That certainly got the staff's attention. All chitchat and fiddling with electronic devices stopped instantly.

They convened around a coffee table on the couches and overstuffed chairs. A girl who looked too young to be in charge of a meeting of anything but a squad of cheerleaders looked at Nick and said, "Okay, so give me your elevator pitch."

Her request was greeted with befuddled silence.

"Your sound bite?"

Nick remained unable to speak. The request obviously baffled him. Twelve years working alone in his frigid basement home office in Cleveland apparently made it difficult to condense his findings into a single sentence. Of course he'd had no time to prepare, he'd been heavily drugged quite recently, was agoraphobic even on a good day, and he'd had very little time to recover from a harrowing near death experience of skydiving sans parachute.

Phoebe tried to help. "As I understand it," she said, "he's discovered a root cause of war."

Several of the media team nodded as they typed on tiny keyboards or used stylish styluses to scribble on screens. "Go on," urged X.

Phoebe looked at Nick, hoping he'd pick up the ball, but he didn't.

"He knows how to prevent wars in the future, too," Phoebe said. "It has something to do with taxes."

"Tariffs," Nick corrected.

Phoebe could feel the interest level plummet. It was as if the room temperature had suddenly dropped forty degrees. Before they were all rendered insensible by the cryo-freeze of boredom she rushed to add, "He's apparently right because people are trying to kill him."

The room warmed up again immediately, and erupted with excited responses, "Fantastic. That is *so cool*!"

Phoebe gave the team a quick overview of the previous twenty-four hours. Her story was received at face value with unquestioning acceptance. Dropping the name of the *Archangel* was apparently the secret password to being taken very seriously indeed, no matter what you were talking about.

CHAPTER 23

When Phoebe finished, all heads turned toward Nick. He managed to pull himself together enough to stutter out the basics. Then, once he got going, his speech smoothed out. "The American Civil War was *not* fought over the issue of slavery," he said. "It was fought for the purpose of vastly increasing the wealth of a handful of very powerful northern industrialists.

"U.S. iron and steel works and garment makers were not able to compete effectively on the open world market. The British could produce better goods at cheaper prices. Because of this, certain U.S. manufacturers wanted taxes to be placed on imports so their prices would seem competitive.

"This is why the Republican Party was formed."

There was some mumbling under the breath at this, but nobody interrupted Nick.

"People in the South, however, relied on an agricultural economy. The South didn't want tariffs because, to the extent that tariffs went up, cotton prices went down.

"This was because the British came to the U.S. to sell their products—and with the money they made from that—they bought cotton to take back to England.

"The money that tariffs took out of British pockets gave them exactly that much less money to spend on cotton."

Gosh, thought Phoebe, she could actually understand what he was saying now.

"The country would never have gone to war to prop up a few floundering mills in the North, though, so the robber barons had to find an appealing cover story.

"The first assaults on southern agriculture weren't successful. So they shifted tactics and went after the Masons because the opposing presidential candidate was a Mason. When that didn't work either, they attacked the Catholics because the Catholics tended to vote overwhelmingly against them.

"For years, northern factory owners funded media propaganda campaigns to sway the public against the slave states, Masons, and Catholics to try to shift the balance of political power away from the anti-tariff Democrats. They didn't really mean to go to war over it, they just wanted the power to raise taxes."

The media team was scribbling and typing furiously.

"Lewis Tappan, a fellow who had owned stock in woolen mills, was the northern ringleader. Some of the leading politicians didn't perceive the real objective of the scheme at first. When it first started, in 1819, Senator Harrison Gray Otis of Massachusetts, for example, had been puzzled at the sudden flurry of anti-slavery talk in the House of Representatives.

"Why all this fuss over a matter of *little or no importance?*, he wondered. It came to him later in a flash of insight while he was traveling. *I woke as if from a trance*, he said, when he finally recognized what the rhetoric was all about. Anti-slavery agitation was a useful propaganda tool to get the political power to control taxes—the *sceptre*, he called it."

A stillness came over the room when Nick said that. Nobody had ever heard anything like that in a Civics or American History class.

"Abraham Lincoln sent Steve Hurlbut, an old political friend, to study the political situation in the South. Hurlbut investigated and reported back to Lincoln. *They have not gone out over slavery*, he told Lincoln. He explained to the President that the southern people believed in free trade and their reason for wanting to secede was because they were seeking the material prosperity they believed would come with free trade.

"Lincoln didn't think free trade was a very good idea. Although he knew he didn't fully understand it all, his party didn't want free trade and he was pledged to support the party platform."

Nick was clearly on a roll now. He had more than a decade of pent up frustration over this issue.

"There was a stalemate in Congress because even though the slave states were a minority, enough free-traders in the North joined with them to oppose tariff legislation. Every time the North got a tariff bill going, the South would kill it. Then things began to get ugly. If the South wouldn't vote for tariffs, the North would foment anti-slavery agitation and vote for abolition.

"Many people in the South were terrified that northern anti-slavery propaganda might cause a slave revolt. Two-thirds of the population of Haiti had died during the Haitian revolution a few years earlier. The whites who didn't flee the country were eventually executed by the former slaves. Tappan was sending mass mailings of anti-slavery propaganda to the South. He invested large amounts of money printing pamphlets for distribution by his agents.

"In one instance a southern Postmaster read one of those pamphlets and seized it to try to prevent violence. A mob burned the mail sacks. Many of the abolitionists didn't want bloody violence and they pulled back from this sort of thing. But Tappan was determined to forge ahead in his crusade to limit southern political power. He didn't mind fomenting chaos and wasn't concerned about the potential for bloodshed."

Nick stopped and took a drink of coffee. He had everyone's full attention at this point.

"Despite all the revisionist history to the contrary, the reality was that the American Civil war was not fought about slavery. The actual chance of abolition was close to zero. Knowledgeable southern leaders didn't actually fear abolition. There was no chance of it occurring, because it would've required a Constitutional Amendment.

"And there was no majority who would vote for it. There wasn't even a significant minority in Congress who were proposing actual abolition. The politicians were simply getting on the Congressional Record with a lot of rhetoric aimed at restricting the westward expansion of southern slave agriculture. The real reason they did this was because they didn't want the South to get two more senators who could obstruct tariff legislation.

Lincoln was well informed that southern leaders were using the anti-slavery hysteria as a propaganda tool to fire the southern heart and drive the masses toward secession for tariff reasons. He knew this must be true since he and the Republican Party had always said they had no intention of interfering with slavery in the states where it actually existed.

"*They didn't want to actually free the slaves* in the southern slave states because that would've entitled the South to additional tariff-obstructing representatives on the floor of the House. So nobody was going to bring the issue of slavery out for a vote.

"If not for the destructive tariff and the anti-slavery agitation, the southern states would almost certainly have extinguished slavery on their own—as did nearly all other countries around the world. The issue would've been resolved peaceably. Astute southern leaders recognized that the anti-slavery agitation from the North had probably set back the cause of emancipation by half a century."

This was a new idea for Phoebe. And it was sickening. All the suffering had been unleashed by a handful of Yankees wanting to make a few bucks.

"The U.S. was an anomaly in that we had a *war* over slavery. A *million* men were killed or wounded and the South was devastated and slandered. The South has never recovered. Its people have suffered under the propaganda ever since. They've never been allowed to recover from the stink of the lies.

"So the truth is that a lot of the so-called bad guys in history turn out to be good guys. And vice versa. The records got destroyed or falsified retroactively and, as usual, the winners' version is what made it into the history books."

Xander was nodding at this.

"I have detailed charts that show the relationship between tariffs and cotton prices. Within a week of a tariff being imposed, cotton growers suffer financial losses. They can't pay off their loans, and the value of the product they are selling plummets. At the same time their overhead increases because everything made of iron and steel, like plows and nails, has become more expensive.

"These aren't subtle or vague economic tendencies, but ironclad relationships. There is a direct and immediate correlation between wealth for a few families in the North being generated in this particular fashion and financial ruin for the entire South.

"Lincoln began to understand this at the end and realized how he'd been used. That's why he had to die.

"And that's why they want me dead."

There was absolute silence in the room.

"I'm here because no one has ever done enough research to be able to make the proofs before. It's taken me more than a decade to do it. The current generation of industrial looters wants all the documents destroyed. And me with them."

Nick hadn't had much time to reflect on what had been happening to him in the last thirty-six hours, but as he'd spoken he'd begun to get an idea who might've leaked his materials and why. He'd given a summary of his findings to a Nobel Prize winning economist. Nick had asked the man specifically what he thought would happen when the Chinese began to sell cars in the U.S. and the laureate had fobbed him off.

The American automotive manufacturers were already struggling. The threat of competition from China had to be terrifying, especially since the poor U.S. economy was making people less and less able to afford major purchases like cars. Nobody in their right mind would want a war with China, so he added these surmises and concerns to his previous comments.

"Free trade prevents wars," he said. There, he'd finally come up with his sound bite.

The team erupted again into rapid crosstalk using a lot of incomprehensible terminology. The girl in charge had a couple of follow-up questions, and adroitly managed to extract what she needed from Nick. She was so pleased at having coaxed him out of his stupor, she leaned over and patted his knee when she was finished.

That made two strangers who'd done that to him in a single day.

"Don't worry," she said, "You've given us the hooks we need. We'll be able to find an angle that will work well for you. We're *very* good at our jobs."

"You don't have everything yet," Nick said. "You'll need to get in touch with my pizza guy."

That got everyone's attention.

"His name is Tommy Bell. He works at the de Medici Pizza place next door to the Cleveland Clinic, the main hospital downtown, in Ohio. He has the flash drive. It's got the draft manuscript on it. It's the only copy left, I think. They took all the others, as well as all the underlying research materials and notes."

CHAPTER 24

The media team's various electronic devices had been playing a muted symphony throughout the meeting, but something Xander saw on the screen of his phone made him stand up suddenly and say, "Meeting's over. You have to leave *now*."

Phoebe and Nick didn't need to be told twice. They headed for the door. "No, no, no!" shouted X. "Not that way! You'll have to go out the other way."

"Other way?" Nick said, confused.

X pointed to a window. He crossed the room quickly and opened it. Nick and Phoebe looked out at the narrow stone balcony. Xander reached for Phoebe, as if to help her, but she backed away, shaking her head. "I'm afraid of heights. *Really* afraid."

"Out here, *now*," X insisted, "go, go go!"

Phoebe balked, "I can't."

Nick scrambled out the waist-high window and onto the balcony. He turned back to face Phoebe and said, "Come on," in a commanding voice. He held out his hand to her and she felt herself gravitating toward him. "Close your eyes," he barked.

Their roles were suddenly reversed. Phoebe couldn't bear to

climb out the window, but then she imagined herself being thrown from it instead when they were caught by whoever was on their way up. That was the extra motivation she needed to move.

She didn't have time to wonder where Nick's new *take charge* personality had come from before she was manhandled through the opening by Xander on the inside and Nick on the outside. "Sorry," Xander said, "Obviously they had surveillance on this facility."

Phoebe took one last longing look into the room and saw the media team frantically manipulating sections of the bookcases that lined the walls of the room. They were tossing their notes and electronic gear into storage areas that were hidden behind rotating sections of the wall. A woman dressed in a maid's costume burst though the door, and breathlessly announced, "Incoming."

Nick and Phoebe were standing shoulder to shoulder on a balcony so tiny, when they turned their backs to the outside wall of the chateau, their heads rested against the lower edge of the massive slate roof. Now Phoebe could see exactly where they were. They were at the roof level of the highest spire on the house.

Phoebe glanced down and saw a shuttle bus stopped below, discharging visitors at the main entrance directly beneath them. She felt her knees start to give out and knew she was going to faint. Nick took her by the upper arm and held her in a surprisingly strong grip.

"You *must* leave," X said, through the window, "we'll buy you as much time as we possibly can."

Phoebe thought they *had* left. Nick glanced around, equally baffled.

"Your best shot is to try for the observation platform," X said, pointing to a railed deck that wasn't more than three or four feet away horizontally, but was separated from the tiny balcony by a terrifying vertical abyss. Then X closed and locked the window behind them.

As soon as Phoebe steadied herself, but before she had time to say anything, Nick swung one leg over the stone balustrade and reached out and took hold of a nylon-coated stainless steel cable that ran atop a line of stone molding. It was a security cable attached to one of the gargoyles on the roof. He stepped off the balcony and onto a slender ledge of decorative stone molding. He held on to the cable and tiptoed around the jutting corner of the building. Phoebe lost sight of him and totally panicked. But then he poked his head back around the corner so she could see him.

"Look at me," he ordered Phoebe in a forceful tone. "Just keep your eyes on me."

Nick held out a hand to her, but Phoebe didn't budge. Then she heard a loud crashing sound in the room behind her, and shouting. She knew she had to move.

She was shaking so hard she didn't know how she could possible maintain a hold on the cable, but she grabbed it, stepped over the balcony railing and onto the narrow ledge, and went toward Nick. Rather than trying to leap across the gap from a precarious standing start, they were taking the long way, which was about ten feet horizontally on a ledge that was barely a toehold and the drop was … something she couldn't allow herself to think about.

Somehow she managed to follow Nick around the corner of the building, having an out of body experience the whole time. By the time she made rounded the corner, she saw that he'd already climbed up onto the wooden observation deck that was built atop the flat roof of a round tower. He leaned over the railing and held his hands out to her.

She looked up at him and saw that he wasn't alone on the platform. A group of tourists were out there too, enjoying the view. Several of them appeared to be taking photos and video of the unexpected acrobatics demonstration. *Circ de Middle-Age*, Phoebe thought.

With a one-handed death grip on the slender cable, she stepped from one narrow ledge cattycorner across the abyss onto another. Nick grabbed her by the wrists and hoisted her across the railing of the rooftop observation deck with the assistance of a fit looking young man who was obviously amused at their antics.

A docent was coming their way shouting, "You must stay with your group! It is not permitted to deviate from the authorized route!"

No kidding, Phoebe thought.

Nick took Phoebe's hand and pulled, "This way," he said, dragging her forcefully behind him as he bolted across the observation platform and headed toward a door that looked like it would lead back into the attic.

They had no idea where they were going as they ran. Phoebe was aware of a blur of verdigris copper, dark gray slate, and blue sky. The view was amazing. You could see for miles. Within a minute they were through the door and back inside the house, in a different part of the attic than they'd been in before, running.

Nick had never visited the house before, so he had no idea about which direction to run. *Down* seemed like reasonable choice. It had been so long since Phoebe had toured the chateaux she had only the foggiest notion of the layout. It seemed like they'd opened a lot more of the house to the public since she'd been there, too, like the observation deck.

Nick stopped suddenly and Phoebe slammed into his back. He reversed course and ran back the way they'd come, pulling her behind him.

Suddenly he hesitated, turned a knob on a three-quarter sized door set into the wall, and shoved Phoebe through it into a cupboard. He joined her and closed the door behind him, putting them in total darkness, smashed together tightly face-to-face.

The hand Nick had used to pull the door closed was trapped behind his back. His other hand was trapped between his body and Phoebe's. They were both as still as possible, but breathing hard.

Nick's injured shoulder was killing him with his hand twisted behind his back. He was afraid to move, though, for fear of jolting the door open.

Phoebe's back was being crushed against the sharp edges of wooden shelving at her shoulders, mid-back, and thighs.

Nick slowly extricated the hand that was trapped between them and then he rested it against the edge of a shelf beside Phoebe's head. He couldn't actually see her, but it was obvious where all her parts were.

He wanted to cry from the pain in his shoulder. In fact, he could hear a faint whine in his breathing that was actually suppressed sobs trying to get out. Being a man was hard. He bent his head to rest it against the shelf and felt Phoebe's hair and the side of her face.

She felt the side of his face, too. He was sandpapering her with his attractive, but scratchy stubble. They were extremely aware of each other, but listened intently as several pairs of heavily shod feet pounded down the hall. Fortunately the feet continued past them without slowing down and kept going until they were no longer audible.

When the sound of the footfalls receded, Nick managed to twist his agonized wrist enough to open the door. He used his good hand to pull Phoebe out into the hall and they started running again. "Somehow we have to get to the garage," he said.

Phoebe agreed, but it was a *long* way from the attic to the lowest of the sub-basements.

CHAPTER 25

Their speed was making them a spectacle, particularly since Nick and Phoebe were racing in the opposite direction of the hordes of tourists being shepherded through the house. But by the time anyone noticed them, they were gone.

They ran down a narrow service staircase that descended only one flight and then gave onto an expansive reception area. Nick did a 360, made a decision, and dragged Phoebe into a sprint toward a massive central staircase. It was a curving masterpiece, made of limestone. But, just as they would've started down, they glanced into the open stairwell and saw two men running up. The men were clearly not tourists. The four of them saw each other at the same time.

The grand staircase was lined with leaded glass windows that would open. They gave access to a highly decorative but mostly useless exterior spiral staircase of carved stone. Nick unlatched a window and climbed through it. *Not again*, Phoebe thought, but she followed him without argument. They tripped down the extremely narrow curved exterior staircase, then crouched behind the waist-high stone wall as their pursuers ran past them, headed upward, without realizing that Nick and Phoebe were hiding just on the other side of the wall.

They were only able to make it down one flight before the exterior stairs came to a dead end against a cold stone wall. Of course it did, it was ornamental. Nick peeked through the lowest window they could reach, then opened it, crawled through, and helped Phoebe clamber inside. He steadied her enough to break her fall as she dropped onto the wide limestone treads of the vast central staircase.

Several tourists goggled at them, surprised to see anyone climbing in via a window. But Nick didn't hesitate. The instant Phoebe was on her feet, he resumed a fast pace down the stairs, moving awkwardly against the tide of visitors.

They fled toward the back of the house, and made it into what, from its narrowness and lack of ornamentation, seemed to be another servant's hallway. It was then that they realized they'd made a serious mistake. There were men running toward them from both directions. Phoebe cast about for options and saw they were standing beside a servants' balcony with a high view into the majestic Banqueting Hall. Unfortunately the drop from there to the floor was at least forty feet.

There was no choice. Nick shoved her to one side and stepped over the rail onto yet another decorative ledge of carved stone. This time there was no cable for a handhold, and the length of travel was much farther, but this ledge was considerably wider than the other one had been. Nick reached back for Phoebe, smiled, and said, "Buck up, my girl. Compared to the last one, this one's a cinch."

Phoebe made a quick prayer and crossed herself, although she wasn't even a Catholic, and began the long traverse, creeping along a four-inch wide path toward the opposite side of the huge room. If they could make it, it would be easy to hop down onto the open gallery that housed the keyboard for a pipe organ that filled the opposite end of the room.

From there, a heavily carved wooden spiral stairway was in plain sight. It ran from the organ loft to the floor. Once they made it down that, they'd be on the ground level and would have a lot of options.

Their movement along a ledge that was more than thirty feet above the heads of the crowd of tourists viewing the room understandably attracted a great deal of attention. Even though photography was forbidden inside the house, camera flashes were going off right and left.

There were a lot of sounds of surprise and also some shouting coming from below, but Phoebe tried to ignore it. She kept her face toward the wall and gripped whatever meager handholds she could find.

Nick talked to her in a steady and encouraging way as they travelled along the ledge. She marveled at his new superhero persona. She had to admit that it hadn't been fair to judge him by how he reacted immediately after being tossed out of a helicopter. He'd been in shock and pain, and then heavily drugged, and dragged through a kaleidoscope of bizarre environments, none of which presented a reasonable opportunity to assess his character. But this guy, … this guy was *feisty*. He was making this almost *fun*.

She felt like she was in a remake of *To Catch a Thief*. If only this was a movie, there'd be stuntmen to do this scene.

Just as they reached the organ loft, their plan to use the stairs from there to the ground was trashed by a man who leaped off the same viewing balcony Phoebe and Nick had climbed out of. Except he flung himself hard in the opposite direction. He didn't go toward the wall and the ledge, he went for the massive sloping hood of the triple-wide fireplace that filled most of that end of the Banqueting Hall and did an acrobatic slide down the face of it like an Olympic luge run.

He skidded down on his rear end, feet first and then was spit out onto the near end of the long, magnificent dining table. He landed on his back, but jumped to his feet and sprinted down the center of the antique table. Clearly he'd be waiting for them at the foot of the stairs by the time they got there.

Another of their pursuers began the precarious ledge walk along the same route they'd taken, so they couldn't go back the way they came.

There was nothing they could do but dash across the organ loft, step up onto the ledge, and head back down the long axis of the room, but this time on the opposite side. Nick couldn't see any way out from there, but there was nowhere else to run.

At this point it was becoming apparent to the rapidly growing audience in the enormous room that several large dangerous-looking men were chasing an obviously terrified middle-aged couple who seemed to be running for their lives.

Human nature being what it is, the spectators couldn't resist taking sides, and without any overt consultation with each other, they sided with the underdogs.

The man running down the long dining table was already experiencing the verbal wrath of the docents, but now he was about to learn a lesson he'd never forget. There are few things on earth more formidable than an angry woman with broom.

A little silver-haired tour guide reached behind a heavy brocaded curtain and came out with a scraggly old wooden-handled broom She swung it, aiming for the man's ankles, with the force and accuracy of a professional baseball player.

The fool with the temerity to damage her beloved dining table went down, hard. When Phoebe saw the havoc that small elderly woman was able to wreak with her humble weapon, against a mercenary, she suddenly grasped the staying power of the iconic image of a woman flying on a broom.

Phoebe wondered why the men didn't just shoot her and Nick. She had no way to know that her pursuers were under revised orders to take the targets alive and with as little controversy as possible. What the men had assumed would be a simple task was getting harder by the minute, especially now that they had hundreds of tourists to contend with as well.

The chateau visitors jostled, shoved, and elbowed them at every opportunity. And by this time, the room was so crowded that people who weren't intentionally trying to disrupt the chase were helping by simply standing in the way. Phoebe silently thanked each of them.

CHAPTER 26

Phoebe and Nick had made it less than halfway along the ledge when Nick noticed that there were latches on the lowest panels of the tall windows that filled the top half of the wall on either side of the Banqueting Hall. He was able to observe them at them at point blank range as he shuffled along the ledge. He realized that, unlike the windows on the other side, these could be opened.

He refocused his eyes and peered through the glass. He realized he was seeing an expanse of roof just outside that was at eye level. Phoebe noticed that Nick had stopped and was looking at something. She stood on tiptoe so she could follow his gaze. It was the roof of the Winter Garden. It was the lowest elevation rooftop in the entire chateau. At its center it had a bulging glass crown that allowed sunlight to shine onto a greenhouse in the atrium of the house called the Palm Court.

Whoever it was who built this pile, Nick thought, thank God he was a stickler for ventilation, or for giving access to window washers. This move was going to be tricky, though—the toughest one yet. The wall was chest high and his shoulder was killing him. Clearly he'd injured it in the fall. All the athletics since then had exacerbated the problem and the chase had metabolized the last of his pain medicine.

Nick held onto the window ledge with one hand and used the other to open the latch. Then he took a deep breath, braced himself inwardly and outwardly, mustered all his focus, and hoisted himself partially through the opening. He had a few terrifying moments kicking against the air as he squirmed his way painfully across the metal edge of the window frame, but he made it through.

He lay on the roof, panting, nearly hysterical. He rested for several seconds, trying to calm himself, then crawled around to face the window and knelt in front of the opening. He reached into the room to take hold of Phoebe's wrists. Then, despite the screaming pain in his shoulder, and an embarrassing howl from his own lips, he lifted her out onto the roof.

They sat clinging to each other for a few seconds, dazed, then looked around. They were back outside, still on the roof, but this time they were two stories closer to the ground. From here it was only about twenty feet down to the cobbled driveway. Nick scrambled to his feet and cast about frantically, hoping to see some way to get down there that wouldn't end in them breaking their necks, but there was nothing.

They had to keep moving, though, so he trotted across the copper roof as it curved around the protruding glass ceiling. On the other side were windows that led back into the house. He hoped these windows would take them into an area that wasn't easily accessible from the Banqueting Hall.

Phoebe got unsteadily to her feet and even though she was wobbly, she carefully followed Nick around the edge of the glass to the other side of the Winter Garden roof.

The chateau was a rabbit warren of eccentric wings and towers. That was both the good news and the bad news. Their progress was now the subject of tremendous interest on the part of not only the bad guys, but also the tourists, and especially the house staff. The astonishing chase through the Banqueting Hall had created a spectacle and their movement around the edge of the glass roof was visible to everyone coming in the main entrance of the house as well as the crowd inside, directly below them, because the Winter Garden faced onto the main ticket counter.

Dozens of rapt faces could be seen upturned, watching in amazement as Nick and Phoebe trotted along the roof. The crowd was now definitely on their side. The tourists had become an outraged mob running fierce interference on Nick and Phoebe's behalf. That turned out to be a real blessing because when they arrived at the windows opposite the Banqueting Hall they discovered there were no latches on the outside.

They were locked out. This made sense, of course. They were on the roof, not a balcony or a staircase, so in ordinary life, no one would be standing where they were, unless they'd come out through a window to perform some maintenance task. And in that case, they'd be able to go back inside the house the same way they'd come out.

But Phoebe and Nick stood, holding hands, gasping for breath, staring at the locked windows. Phoebe had to lean against the wall for support. Nick looked at her in despair. He'd failed her. They were going to get caught.

He decided to kick one of the windows in, but then he heard some muffled voices and the click of a latch. A window near where they were standing opened wide and the heads of two children popped out. A pre-teen boy and girl waved extravagantly in the universal gesture of, *Over here!*

Not another freaking window, Phoebe thought, but she was nevertheless grateful for the help and she followed Nick as he crawled through and dropped onto the floor of a bedroom. The children and their mother were giggling and happy to be participating in the game, whatever it was.

"Thanks," Nick gasped.

The room had several doors, each leading to parts unknown. "Stairs?" he asked.

The children's mother pointed at one of the doors. Nick and Phoebe were both winded, but their run had gone on long enough at this point to release endorphins, so now they were both high as well. *This would make a heck of a weight loss boot camp,* Phoebe thought. If she survived, maybe she'd mention it to the Chateau St. Cloud marketing people.

They left by the door indicated and dashed across another of the open reception areas that bordered each landing for the grand central staircase. This time they made it down to the ground.

CHAPTER 27

At that point they would've run out the front door, but an elderly female guide moved as if to block their way and made an emphatic gesture toward the back corner of the chateau. In fact, she jogged ahead of them, leading them into a majestic two-story library with a mezzanine level balcony that ran around the perimeter of the room in a much larger version of the one where they'd met with the media people.

The docent led them up a carved wooden staircase to the balcony and opened a panel that allowed them to stand out of sight in a space behind the fireplace flue. They stepped into the dark space and the lady closed the door on them. They heard her light footfalls as she descended the stairs.

This hideaway was plenty large enough for Nick and Phoebe to sit down in. They sat side by side on the floor. It was oddly reminiscent of the darkroom, Phoebe thought. Once her eyes adjusted to the gloom, she could make out the fact that there was a door on either side of the little room. She supposed this was to allow passage around the room on the balcony level. It was a way to walk behind the chimney so you wouldn't have to take the stairs down to the ground level and then climb back up on the other side of the fireplace.

Rich people, Phoebe thought.

They were both sweating and breathing hard. Nick lay down and stretched out on his back. Phoebe did the same. They were both trying to be as still and quiet as possible. Phoebe turned her head to look at him. There was just enough light coming in from underneath the doors, to see each other.

She couldn't decide whether Nick looked disreputable or handsome, or both. Before she realized what was happening, he leaned over and kissed her.

At that same moment they heard several sets of running heavy footfalls burst into the room. They both froze, their faces remaining at point blank range as they listened to the docent ask in a thin pedantic old lady voice if the visitors would like to hear the history of the library.

Apparently these particular visitors weren't interested. The clomping of boots continued through the room and left by a side door that was on the main tour route.

A minute later Nick and Phoebe heard a loud, *Pssst.* Nick crawled over to the door and silently opened it just a crack. He peeked out and the old lady gestured with both arms, like a traffic cop, to indicate they should come down the stairs and then go out through the French doors on the opposite side of the room.

Nick and Phoebe quickly made their way down the staircase and passed through the French doors the docent unlocked for them. They found themselves on a loggia at the back of the house. There was a stupendous, life-changing panorama of immaculate rolling lawns bordered by vast artistically arranged forests, and rows of blue mountains beyond. The view was heart-stopping. So was the drop.

"Oh joy," said Nick, as he leaned over the loggia balustrade and took in the sheer stone wall, forty or fifty feet to the immaculately maintained lawn behind the house.

"It is recommended that you not attempt to reach the garage and the vehicle you arrived in," the old woman said, "but instead make your way round to the front of the chateau. There will be cars available there." Then she pointed to a heavy-duty copper drainpipe that was held onto the wall with sturdy copper clamps. It ran in a straight line from the roof down the entire back of the house, passing within inches of the loggia railing.

Nick smiled at the woman, then he swept her up into a romantic embrace and kissed her on the lips with a loud smacking sound. "Thank you," he said, obviously meaning it.

Phoebe was wondering what had gotten into him, but didn't have time to ask before he stepped over the balustrade and gripped the sides of the drainpipe. He turned a pirate's smile on her, said, "Follow me," and began a long careful slide toward the ground.

As soon as Phoebe's feet touched the ground they started a long sprint around the side of the gigantic house and uphill toward the parking area at the front.

"Well, that was fun," Nick wheezed. "I've always wanted to see the chateau."

Phoebe burst out laughing, even though she could hardly breathe. Her lungs were on fire. Now that they were running across the grass, the horror of heights left her. She realized Nick was great fun. Phoebe hadn't had fun in a *long* time. She'd spent the last few years getting old instead.

Now she realized that even though her lifespan might be considerably shorter than she'd previously imagined, at least she'd enjoy the time left to her.

That seemed like a fair trade.

CHAPTER 28

Because they'd arrived from the back and been preoccupied since then, Phoebe and Nick had no idea that an antique car show and rally was getting set up around the edges of the formal driveway in front of the house. As they burst around the corner and ran along the parterre, they became aware of the dozens of restored antique convertibles lining the drive. The splendid cars were backed in so the grilles faced out. Proud owners stood nearby in period costume.

Phoebe jogged past the automobiles reading the names drawn in florid script on small cardboard signs that rested against the windshield of each car. Most of them were brands she'd never heard of: Berliet, Amilcar, Delaugère Clayette & Cie, Ballot, Chenard-Walcker, Cottin & Desgouttes, and De Dion-Bouton. Phoebe adored cars, especially ones like these. She much rather have a vintage vehicle than jewelry or furs. She never wore jewelry and was a vegetarian, but she did drive, a lot.

Phoebe slowed down and got practical. She checked each car she race-walked passed it to see how the floor pedals were configured, if the vehicle required a metal crank to be started, if it required a key, and, if so, was the key in the ignition.

She formulated a plan. She continued down the row of cars, scanning another group of vehicles: Turcat Méry, Doriot Flandrin

Parant, Rayet-Liénart, Hotchkiss, Mors, Sizaire Fréres et Naudin, and Unic. The value of each car was written at the bottom of each placard. The numbers were in five figures.

Phoebe veered toward a car that's engine happened to be running. The vehicle was a bizarre concoction of wood in the shape of a boat mounted on a rolling chassis. She checked the floor. It was a right hand drive, but had three normal looking foot pedals. The one on the right was long and narrow, the two on the left were square-ish and the same size.

In a flash she leaped into the driver's seat. She literally had to leap because the car had no doors. She shouted to Nick, "Get in!"

He did a double take, then ran around to the other side, stepped up on the running board, and hopped in. Phoebe put the car in gear and floored it. In mere seconds she'd cleared the tall gates at the entrance to the chateau. Nick got himself settled in the passenger seat and looked for a seatbelt. There wasn't one.

In the rear view mirror Phoebe could see bemused spectators, smiling tourists who were waving at them in delight, and an enraged couple in costume who were attempting to give chase on foot. She was relieved to note there were no henchpersons in sight.

Just as the splendid car raced away, three men dressed in black jumpsuits emerged from behind the house barely in time to see Nick and Phoebe disappear into the decorative forest that surrounded the estate.

Phoebe's friends were convened around the biggest table in White Oak at the café in Hamilton's Store: Leon, Ivy, Waneeta, Jill, Doc, Lester, and Fate.

Jill, the owner, set a plate of deviled eggs in the middle of the table along with a pitcher of sweet tea. "If you want anything else, get it yourself," she said, and took a seat.

Leon, Ivy, and Waneeta filled everyone in on the parts of the story they knew. They had no idea where Phoebe's new job was, or if she'd been able to show up for it.

"What next?" Doc asked. Now retired, he'd been Phoebe's mentor since she was a little girl.

"Let's all just sit tight close to a phone at our usual hangouts and wait. I'm pretty sure one of us'll be gittin a call before too long," said Lester. Since Lester and Fate were professional criminals, they were the experts in this kind of situation. Everyone nodded at Lester's sensible advice, then the meeting broke up and they all went their separate ways.

Phoebe and Nick gained a considerable lead thanks to their spur of the moment grand theft auto. They were miles from the chateau by the time their pursuers were able to regroup and recalibrate. They were helped by the chateau guards who locked the main gates as soon as they realized one of the antique cars had been stolen.

Nick twisted around and rummaged in the back seat of the boatmobile. He retrieved a magnificent wide brim hat with feathers on it. He offered it to Phoebe, but she shook her head. Next he held out a vintage Hermes scarf. She took that asked him to steer while she tied it around her head Grace Kelly style. She suspected at her age she actually looked more like the Queen, but she still enjoyed wearing a $300 scarf.

She put her hands back on the steering wheel and next Nick flourished an extremely elegant pair of round retro sunglasses. She put those on, too.

He waved a pair of old-style driving gauntlets toward her but she shook her head. Nick tossed the feathered hat into the back with the gloves, a pair of antique driving goggles, and a flat tweed cap.

The windshield of the car was made of two horizontal pieces of glass. The top half was capable of being tilted like a louver to create an opening between the two halves. Old school air-conditioning, Nick presumed, although it was plenty windy with it closed. The view on his side was being blocked by a cardboard placard, so he raised up and reached across the top of the windshield and plucked the sign out from underneath a windshield wiper.

He read the text to himself, then said to Phoebe, "You have stolen a 1914 Rolls-Royce Silver Ghost Boat-Tail Skiff."

They exchanged bemused smiles. Despite their desperate circumstances, Phoebe felt younger than she had in years. Nick resumed reading the description of the car aloud.

"'The Silver Ghost was the most comfortable luxury car ever built and the only one available that was quiet enough to allow for normal conversation at speed. The automobile ran in complete silence without a puff of smoke—a feat that could not be matched at the time and has never been duplicated since.'"

The engine *was* extremely quiet, but road noise and wind sounds were still there.

"'The construction of skiff bodies on an automobile chassis was primarily a French innovation,'" Nick continued. "'Boat-shaped automobiles were designed specifically to cheat the wind.'"

"Love that old language," Phoebe sighed. "It's so poetic. I've heard the phrase *land yacht*, but I never realized somebody had actually made one. Or that I'd be driving it!"

"Blah, blah, blah ... something about steam power, quadricycles, and flying tricycles," Nick said. "Bottom line, this baby has 48 horsepower and will go 75 miles an hour."

"Quadricycles?" Phoebe asked.

"We're in one," Nick said, " a vehicle with four wheels. I guess they didn't call them *cars* yet."

"Flying tricycles?"

"You got me there. Hey, here's something that explains why this thing looks like a boat. Some fabulously rich rowing fanatic went to a car maker—at the turn of the century it was apparently common for rich people to have custom cars manufactured to order—and the guy told the car maker, 'Make me a torpedo without doors.'

"'But how will you get in?' asks the car maker."

"'One will step over,' says the rich guy."

"'And the ladies?' asks the car maker."

"'Well, they will also step over,' says the rich guy. 'We will finally see their legs!'"

Phoebe snorted, and thought, but didn't say aloud, *Men. Where all lines of thought eventually converge on women's body parts.* Men had their own idiotic variation of non-Euclidean geometry.

"So," Phoebe said, "some French guy was rich enough to

commission the only car in the world that was silent and built almost exactly like a boat so he could sail on dry land at 75 miles an hour and maintain civilized conversation."

They traded a quick glance with raised eyebrows.

"Not a French guy. This particular car was owned by a gentleman from Cairo," Nick said, then set the placard in the footwell of the back seat.

"Do you think they're still following us?" Phoebe asked.

"Oh, I'm certain of it," Nick said. He took a long look at Phoebe in her scarf and sunglasses. She was the picture of chic, vintage adventure.

"I don't understand why they didn't shoot us. Don't they wanna kill you, or do you think they intend to torture you first?"

Nick drew a deep breath and pondered her question. "I believe we can feel fairly certain they intended to kill me—based on the whole throwing-me-out-of-the-helicopter episode. I suppose they were reluctant to shoot us in front of all those people at St. Cloud. But now I've embarrassed them by remaining alive several times despite their best, highly professional, efforts.

And, of course, now they'll be annoyed with you, too. Being outwitted, humiliated in public, by a woman is bound to get on the nerves of even the most egalitarian male assassin. So, I'd say the odds favor at least a modicum of torture, and then death, for us both."

They each thought about that, but were surprised to find it didn't really frighten them as much as perhaps it should. They'd exhausted their *fight or flight* hormones at this point. Nothing was particularly scary any more, at least while they were on the ground, at least for a while.

"The new development is that I'm pretty sure we've got new set of pursuers now."

"Why?" asked Phoebe.

"Because this car, the one you stole, is worth $1.2 million dollars."

CHAPTER 29

Phoebe stiffened her arms, leaned back as far as possible, and took her foot off the gas. The car rolled a long way, then gradually came to a stop. She looked at Nick slack-jawed.

"Oh. My. God," she said. "I think I'm gonna throw up."

She stood up so she could clamber out of the doorless car. Then she got out as carefully as she could, trying not to scratch anything.

"We can't just stop," Nick said. "We have to keep going."

Phoebe shook her head violently and then burst into tears. She was horrified at what she'd done. Phoebe was crazy about cars. She couldn't believe she'd raced off in a one-of-a-kind museum piece. An irreplaceable bit of automotive history.

How could she, on her first attempt, have stolen one of the most expensive cars in the whole wide world? She'd *never* be able to forgive herself. She'd never be able to pay for the damage either.

Her life was ruined. How could she have been so stupid. She'd gone insane. That's what a few moments of fun would get you every time. Regret. And years of incarceration.

"I … can't," she said, holding a hand over her mouth. "I can't hurt it any worse than I already have. These roads," she waved her hand, "are too rough for .... ."

"Then I'll drive," Nick said easily, and he moved over into the driver's seat. He rummaged in the back seat for male attire, then slipped the Red Baron goggles on, donned the leather gauntlets, slapped the flat cap atop his head, and took hold of the steering wheel with gusto. "Come on, old girl," he said. "Can't have you losing heart now."

Phoebe took her shoes off and carefully stepped over the side of the boat body and into the passenger side. Her nose was still red from crying. Nick put the car in gear and took off as if he didn't have a care in the world.

"Out of all those cars, why did I have to pick *this* one?" Phoebe moaned. "I didn't mean to. I did it because I was afraid we wouldn't be able to steal any of the ones that weren't already running. I don't know how to crank start a car, do you?"

"Nope," said Nick, smiling, obviously enjoying himself. He'd been smiling continuously since they'd stolen the car.

After a few minutes Phoebe realized it, and said, "You're a really good driver."

"I used to drive a lot, professionally," he said.

"You were truck driver?" Phoebe asked. She couldn't picture it, but of course she didn't know him, not really. "Why'd you quit?" Phoebe asked.

She wondered if it had to do with the agoraphobia, which he seemed to be totally over, probably on account of some inability of the human brain to stack more than half a dozen death scenarios at a time, combined with adrenal exhaustion.

"I got tired of it," he said. "I mean how many times do you need to drive around in a circle until you grasp the concept?"

"What?"

Then he pressed harder on the gas, and said, "I drove racecars."

It took a few minutes for Phoebe to adjust to riding in a $1.2 million museum exhibit piloted by a singularly strange stranger who'd just confessed to being a racecar driver.

She considered his rhetorical question about how many times a person had to go around a track to learn a concept, and had to admit that she'd been going around and around the same, or similar, tracks for most of her life and she still didn't understand much.

Phoebe didn't know what to think about anything anymore. The longer she lived, the fewer opinions she had. Life was complicated and we all came into it totally inexperienced. The older she got, the more she resisted second-guessing herself or anyone else. You did the best you could, then you moved on. End of post-game critique.

She looked out at the passing landscape. What a paradise. And riding in an open top car, made it even nicer. "I'm not sure what this says about my life," Phoebe said, "but I've gotta admit, being chased by homicidal maniacs with you is more fun than any date I've ever been on."

He shot her a glance, gave her a rakish smile, and said, "What if this *is* my idea of a date?"

Gradually, as Nick drove masterfully through the woods at speed, Phoebe pulled herself together and began to relax. She removed the cell phone from of the little bag she was wearing on a lanyard under her tunic and was thrilled to discover it still worked even after all her hijinks.

Waneeta's answering machine picked up and Phoebe left a message requesting a callback immediately.

Next she dialed Lester.

Lester was the head of the two-man crime wave that was headquartered in White Oak, the tiny rural Tennessee mountain community where Phoebe lived. Lester ran the biggest car theft ring in the southeast. He was also a sociopath. But, for reasons known only to God, he liked Phoebe and was always nice to her. He'd come through for her before in an awkward and dangerous situation, so she knew she could count on him if she needed his help again.

Lester's main office was in an old Esso Station that he'd spared no expense in restoring to its original condition. The station didn't actually sell gas, but sometimes you could wangle permission to use the pristine antique pump, just to keep it in working condition. But you had to pay the going rate rather than the 31¢ a gallon it was set at.

Thinking about the Esso station reminded Phoebe that she had no idea how much fuel was in the million dollar car. She wasn't sure if it had a gas gauge. She didn't even know if it ran on gas. Oh, well, it was too late to worry about that now. She hoped they had enough to make it to wherever they were going. If only she knew where that was.

One thing she did know was that Lester and his boys were gonna love this car.

Fate, Lester's second in command, answered the phone at the Esso station. "Where are ye?" he asked.

Phoebe tried to explain her situation to him as quickly as possible with a minimum of emotional content or babbling. Early in her narrative he interrupted her to say, "Puttin you on speaker so Lester can hear."

Otherwise neither of the men said anything to stop her from describing what was going on and asking for their advice and help.

"You need to get to the national forest," Fate said, when she was finished speaking. "Yer right on the edge of it now. If ye can git into there, there's all kinda loggin roads. They'll never be able to foller ye if ye've got a good lead."

"Talk fast," Nick warned. "As soon as we top this ridge, we may lose the connection."

Fate explained the route he wanted Phoebe to take. She repeated everything he said to Nick, so he could help her remember.

"We'll head your way now," Fate said. "If ye can stay ahead of em for an hour, we'll take over from there and handle things. Do ye think ye can do that?

"I don't know," Phoebe said, "We have a good lead now, but I'm not sure how long it'll last. We'll give it our best shot."

She heard Lester say something in the background and the speakerphone went off. Lester said, "Give me your cell number."

Lester and Fate were already on the move. If there was one thing hoods loved, it was a fight.

CHAPTER 30

The Gryphon glared at his subordinates and said menacingly, "If this gets out...." He left the rest of his threat to their imaginations.

He paced in front of the wall of glass, oblivious to the spectacular panorama of Central Park. "This can *not* get out," he said, with emphasis.

"Don't worry," his lieutenant said, "It's too complicated. People are too lazy to focus on anything this arcane. There's no entertainment value."

"What's the entertainment value of anything on television these days?" the Gryphon responded.

"You're right, sir, of course, I should have said that the sort of sex and violence and lifestyles of the rich and trashy that are successful now, are a far cry from post-graduate level economics and ugly moments in history that are best left forgotten. This guy has no financial resources, no media platform, and no friends."

"Then how did he escape from an aircraft *in flight* nude and without a parachute? How is that even possible?" He slapped his desk with an open hand making a sharp crack, then he screamed, "How is that possible!"

The Chief of Security stepped forward and assumed the rigid stance the military used to simulate relaxation and said, "Sir, there is no way this man can survive."

"Where is he now?" he asked, giving his security chief a hard stare.

"He's in the Appalachian Mountains near the border between North Carolina and Tennessee. We're about to regain his position. Then we'll handle him. This will be over within the hour."

When he was back in his own office, the security chief smirked and said, "There's no way a bunch of hillbillies can win this."

"You'd better be careful," his lieutenant warned. "The mountains breed *fierce* people. And their home terrain is naturally defensible."

He flipped a switch that illuminated a screen mounted on the wall. He clicked some keys on a wireless keyboard and a world map appeared. Then he made some hand gestures in the air that set various markers on the screen.

"Consider the European Micro-States like Andorra, Liechtenstein, Malta, Monaco, San Marino, Luxembourg, and Cyprus. Mountains define these places. Think of the intractable wars in Afghanistan, Tibet, Kashmir, the Caucasus, Rwanda, and the Nuba Mountains in Sudan. Do *not* underestimate your opponents."

If he'd been smarter he'd have added Ireland and Scotland into that list of irascible and intractable foes. A dozen generations of these feisty souls had been born and raised in Appalachia and now a handful of their most outstandingly reactive descendants were blithely awaiting his arrival.

CHAPTER 31

Nick and Phoebe were lucky in so many respects. It was a glorious summer afternoon and the car was running perfectly. After they located and made the first crucial turn off the hardtop road and onto a dirt logging road that led into the Pisgah National Forest, they both felt considerably safer.

Although the tall wheels on the car gave them excellent ground clearance, they had to slow down on the narrow uneven surface. But even at the reduced speed, they were still making good time.

Phoebe knew her friends would be hurtling toward them. She didn't know who the people were who were after Nick, but she knew one thing for certain, they were no match for Lester and Fate.

Angry Appalachians were justifiably world famous for their ability to create mayhem. The White Oak area was the Afghanistan of the Western World. It had been invaded several times and was occupied by two alien forces at the moment—the National Park Service and retirees from Michigan—but they'd never be conquered.

Fate had given clear instructions, so Nick and Phoebe were able to maintain a relatively steady heading for the crucial hour he'd asked them to give him.

"There they are!" Phoebe shouted, as she pointed to the two

pieces of heavy equipment beside the road up ahead of them. There was a track hoe with pincers and a ferocious looking machine with jaws and a saw on a boom. This was heavy-duty commercial logging equipment. Phoebe assumed it belonged to the company that had the contract with the government to log the area.

She raised up off her seat and waved over the top of the windshield, making the special redneck call local women used to be heard across long distances or over the roar of farm equipment. A generic name for the sound might be a yodel or hog call, but it was mostly used to call men in from a field for their meals or to get someone's attention if you needed to warn them.

Men tended to use the piercing whistle made by putting their tongue against their front teeth, but despite many years of trying Phoebe had never been able to lean to whistle like that. Lester and Fate waved back from atop the well-used yellow Caterpillar warhorses.

Phoebe was constantly amazed at the ability the men of her region to drive nearly anything. She had no doubt they could fly the space shuttle if necessary. All the local kids grew up learning to drive on tractors, but then the genders tended to split and the boys progressed until they'd mastered every conceivable sort of motorized transportation. Thinking about this filled her with pride.

Fate signaled for them to keep going and Nick shot through the gap between the roaring machines. The mechanized beasts clattered and growled and then closed the road behind Nick and Phoebe.

They wanted to stop and wait to see what was going to happen, but Fate signaled for them to keep going. If hand gestures could've spoken fluently, his said, *leave now and don't look back.*

They wouldn't have been able to see much anyway because the machines were blocking most of the view, but before they went far, there was a terrible crashing and grinding noise behind them. It was followed by the loud revving of a diesel engine and a horrible pterodactyl-like screeching sound pierced the wilderness.

Despite his instructions, Nick slid to a stop and a cloud of dust boiled up around the car. Phoebe stood up in her seat and looked back in time to see the pinchers grab a black SUV by the roof and lift it off the ground. A hydraulic ax clipped the lower portion of one of the front wheels off, the boom tilted the SUV the other way, and the axe severed the other front wheel.

"My God, it's like watching an Appalachian Transformer movie, but it's *real*!" Phoebe said.

"Monster trucks meet mercenaries," mumbled Nick.

There was a burst of automatic weapons fire, and some screaming.

"Should we go back? Do you think they need us?"

"Nope," said Phoebe. "We better do as we're told."

After the first vehicle was disabled, the track hoe started making its way up onto the hood of the second SUV.

Nick floored the Rolls and tore off through the woods. He drove the little convertible like a professional moonshiner, obviously having a great time.

"Are you enjoying this?" Phoebe asked, incredulous. The escapades with the logging equipment had shocked her back into panic mode.

He nodded and smiled. "Yes! And you know why? Because I'm not dead!" he shouted. "That's great news. And I'm over ... I'm over ...."

He glanced at her, struggling for words.

"What?" she asked.

"Everything!"

"Like what?"

"I didn't get out much. Before."

She suspected that was a massive understatement.

He glanced at her again, clearly hoping for her understanding.

"I didn't get out all, really. But I'm out now, and I'm still breathing, and I'm driving one of the greatest cars on earth, and you're with me, … and it's all good."

When he put it like that, Phoebe had to agree.

CHAPTER 32

They'd made it maybe three miles further along the logging road when they were met by an old Toyota Land Cruiser painted matte black. The driver stuck his head out the window and waved.

"It's Jakey," Phoebe said, "I know him, he works with Lester and Fate."

Jakey got out and walked to the Rolls. Phoebe was torn between shame and pride when she saw the look Jakey gave the car.

"It's a Rolls-Royce," she said proudly. "I stole it."

He gave Phoebe an appraising look and laughed. "Girl, I underestimated you."

He turned back to examine the car more closely. It was utterly incongruous for a vehicle like that to be sitting on a dirt road in the middle of the deep Appalachian woods.

"We thought it'd be best for y'all to switch cars," Jakey said, "just in case. O'course I had no ideal what ye were drivin. Now that I see it, I'm gonna need to modify the plan."

He walked around the car, inspecting it from all sides. "Sister, ye mighta overshot the mark with this'n."

"Whaddya mean?" she asked.

"I'm impressed, I'll give ye that. But a car like this'n's pretty high profile. Ye did a good job gettin her, but we can't let ye keep her. Don't worry, we'll git ya'll outta here but then we're gonna have to put this back where she belongs. I'll wipe her down real good first."

Phoebe glanced back the way they'd come.

"There was quite a bit of racket back there. I hope things are goin okay," said Phoebe, still worried.

Jakey smiled and held up a walkie-talkie and said, "I can guarantee things are goin just fine. Don't you worry about a thing. We'll do a little bit of tidyin here up and then we'll be right behind ya."

"Fate told me to give you this," Jakey said, and handed Phoebe an M-1 carbine loaded with an extended clip. Then he held out two more clips.

"He's so sweet," Phoebe said, and got into the passenger side of the Land Cruiser with the rifle and set the extra ammo in the floor at her feet.

The outside of the Toyota was low-key in the extreme, but it was quite the opposite on the inside. It was pristine.

Nick got in on the driver's side and said, "Where do you people get all these vehicles?"

"It's just part of the local lifestyle. It's how we entertain ourselves. This Land Cruiser is nice, but you haven't lived til you've ridden in an amphibian. Daddy used to have a six-wheel drive ATV called a *Buffalo* – an amphibious vehicle the military uses in the Arctic. That thing would go anywhere."

Jakey waved *bye,* and they waved back.

Nick shook his head as he did a neat three-point turn in the Land Cruiser. Phoebe studied his determined, no-nonsense profile. This was a different guy than the one she'd met the day before. Getting out of the house, or, more specifically, the basement, was good for him.

"Nick nodded toward the rifle and asked, "Do you know how to use that?"

"Very well indeed," replied Phoebe.

"Could you really shoot someone with it?"

"I honestly don't know. I don't think anybody can say ahead of time what they'd do. I know it would be a lot easier to shoot somebody in defense of someone else than it would be to defend myself. But here, when a man hands you a gun, you take it and say *thank you.* This isn't the sort of place where you can have a sane discussion about guns or whether and under what circumstances you might find yourself able to use it."

"You have quite the cadre of friends," Nick said. "Who are they, some sort of militia?"

"Honey, the whole southern Appalachian highlands is one big militia. It always has been. We're born into it. We serve on active duty all our lives—men, women, children, and dogs.

"We don't start wars," she added, "but we do love to participate."

"Do you hear anything?" Phoebe asked.

Nick stopped the car, rolled his window down, and then when he thought he might be hearing something in the distance, switched the engine off.

At first all he heard was wind in the trees, then he began to make out a familiar whomp-whomp-whomp.

A helicopter was coming.

"Oh, *hell* no," he said. "Not again."

He cranked the Land Cruiser and drove it off the road and into the woods, hiding it as well as he could.

The chopper flashed by and kept going without a pause. "Reckon they're lookin for their friends?" Phoebe asked.

"I'd say so."

"*They know not what they do,*" Phoebe quoted.

A few moments later there was an explosion, followed by a shrieking sound, and then another, even bigger explosion.

"What was that?" Nick asked. "Could they have shot the helicopter down?"

Phoebe shrugged.

"Wouldn't you'd have to have a rocket launcher to do something like that!"

Phoebe shrugged again.

Nick said nothing, just pulled out from between the trees and continued down the dirt road headed toward White Oak.

CHAPTER 33

Jill had brought her television into the café and set it up on the counter so everyone could watch it. It was tuned to CNN. "You've gotta see this," she said to Phoebe. "You're not gonna believe it. You two are on the national news. They're talkin about Nick's book."

"Book?" Nick said. "There's no book."

It should've been impossible for the media team to have produced a book in the brief time since he and Phoebe had left Chateau St. Cloud. When he'd been kidnapped from his basement office in Cleveland two days ago, he'd had half a dozen filing cabinets filled to bursting with research notes, countless teetering stacks of paper covering every available surface, and a 2,000 page rough draft manuscript.

Even if the St. Cloud people could've reached Tommy the pizza guy immediately, which was only a few hours ago, all he'd had on the flash drive was the same 600,000 word draft. The greatest editor in the world couldn't have cleaned that manuscript up in a few hours.

"There's no book," Nick repeated adamantly.

"It was on cable first," said Jill, "but now it's on all the regular networks, too. Ya'll have gone viral. They're usin that video of you everywhere like they did that Chinese fella who stood in front of the tank."

"What video?" Phoebe asked. "What's gone viral?"

Doc, the retired local physician, pointed at the screen and said, "That."

Phoebe watched in amazement. What appeared to be a hodgepodge of amateur footage of the chateau and clips from security cameras had been cut together to make a short film that painted the story of their adventure as well as any big-budget Hollywood production ever could have. In fact, this was all the more riveting because it was obviously spontaneous and real.

First there was a wide shot of the chateau to help people understand the size and scale of the place. Then there was the hair-raising scramble out the first window and Phoebe and Nick's walk along the high exterior ledge. It must've been taken by a tourist standing on the front lawn.

Nick's athletic leap and scramble onto the observation platform and subsequent hoisting of Phoebe after him was astonishing, if not exactly flattering to Phoebe. Next came footage of them running through the house while being chased by men wearing body armor.

The footage of their terrifying transit of the ledge inside the Banqueting Hall, first on one side of the long room and then the other, would've been unbelievable, except that it was obviously real. The nearly unbearable tension of the situation was temporarily alleviated by the comic relief of the feisty little gray-haired docent using a mop handle to trip the soldier who was attempting to run the length of the dining table.

There were shaky images of Nick and Phoebe clambering out onto the greenhouse roof, again making Nick look like James

Bond's father and showcasing a not very flattering view of Phoebe's backside.

Then there was a gap in the chase that was obvious to Phoebe and Nick, but not to anyone who hadn't seen it in person. The film jumped to footage of Phoebe and Nick leaping into the Rolls and racing away. This time Phoebe thought she came off looking pretty good. Seeing the people chasing them down the driveway in their glamorous antique motoring costumes made her feel terrible. Stealing the car had been sort of fun in the life and death emergency, but now she felt guilty.

Obviously the *Archangel's* media guys were behind this. They'd somehow collected the snippets and edited them all together to display the whole narrative arc from its startling inception, initial panic, brave and determined flight, to the victorious and stylish escape. Phoebe was forced to congratulate herself for driving away in that antique Rolls Royce. It really put the most elegant possible cap on the entire escapade.

Jill changed the channel and they watched it all again, this time with some of the footage missing from the previous version. Phoebe saw the shadows she and Nick had cast onto startled tourists below as they raced around the glass roof of the Winter Garden before tearing through a series of grandly furnished rooms, leaping red velvet ropes. Then, when you thought it couldn't get any better, they slid three or four stories down a drainpipe, and raced away in the coolest car *ever*.

What helped make the film so riveting was that the heroes were obviously *not* actors or athletes, but instead, a real-life middle-aged man and woman who were clearly running for their lives in a unchoreographed panic. Phoebe had to admit they'd put on quite a show. It was fabulous—even inspiring.

Then an impressive-looking book cover flashed on the screen. The title was *The Last War* and the author was Nick Phélypeaux. "Is *that* your last name?" Phoebe blurted.

Nick nodded.

"How do you even *say* that?"

A ticker tape ran across the lower part of the screen with the name Frederic Nicolas Fulk Phélypeaux-Blaxland de Lalande, Prince de Mars, Duc de Mercœur.

"Uh oh," Nick murmured.

Phoebe looked at the long row of names and the funny mark over the *e* and the hyphen, but she couldn't take it in. The best she could come up with was something like Freddie Mercury. She said, "Your name's got two letters that're stuck together."

He sat stone-faced, staring at the screen.

"How do you say letters when they're stuck together?" Phoebe struggled to make sense of this new development. "Fulk sure sounds like one terrifying kicker of asses."

"He was."

She looked at him, baffled, "Are you really a Prince?"

He didn't respond.

"Of *Mars*?"

Nothing.

"Is that the planet Mars or somewhere else?"

Nick covered his face with his hands.

"And a Duke?" she said, pronouncing it *dooook* in the local dialect with the vowel sound drawn out. The more agitated Phoebe got, the deeper her natural speech went into the archaic dialect. "Whut's zat mean?"

"It indicates that a thousand years ago I had a male ancestor who was remarkably ill-tempered and extremely well-armed."

Phoebe burst out laughing. "Got any castles … on Mars?

Nick still couldn't pull his eyes away from the televised feed, but he said, "Mars is the Roman god of war. His essential characteristics are virility and virtue."

"Virility and virtue, that sounds like a painful combination," Phoebe said.

He pretended not to hear her. "We have half a dozen crumbling piles of stone back in the old country. That would be France, not the planet Mars. They're called *chateaux* as you would know if you'd bothered to read your brochure during our tour of St. Cloud."

CHAPTER 34

"Is that how *Le* Seigneur knew who you were?"

He nodded.

Now she wondered what else was concealed behind her patient's vague *honorific* title. *Steve,* indeed.

"And that's why you're interested in war, because of the French Revolution?"

He shook his head. "My family's problems started long before that. I come from a family of heretics. We're Protestants—Huguenots.

"Our religious eccentricities were tolerated for a while, but the Catholic hard liners would periodically round up anyone who objected to the corruption of the state religion and punish them. Protestants were tortured and burned alive, or hung in the windows of the royal palaces for decoration.

"My line survived because my ancestor happened to be away when the soldiers battered down the door of the family's main residence. After that he made an emergency decision to relocate to another continent."

"Are you rich?"

"Nope. My ancestor was out hunting when all hell broke loose. He came to this country in the late 1600's with the clothes on his back. We've been broke since then."

The news anchor was talking about the leak of a confidential manuscript that had set the publishing world on its ear. Phoebe looked at Nick and he shook his head, mumbling, "Never seen it before."

They sat for an hour and watched endless replays of themselves in fascination.

The Fox news anchor said the book would be available tomorrow. Massive advance orders had driven it to #1 on the *New York Times*, *Wall Street Journal*, and *USA Today* bestseller lists. An unprecedented printing of 500,000 hardback copies was anticipated in light of the substantial public interest.

Nick and Phoebe were a sensation on social media, too. The video of the wild chase and escape was being watched by millions on YouTube. Twitter was flooded with #Roofies, #RocktheChateau and #Democrazy.

The thesis of Nick's book, the actual cause of wars being tariffs that enriched a handful of industrialists, was apparently being summarized succinctly by news commentators in many different languages around the world.

Although very few people, if any, would ever have been able to come up with this economic insight on their own, it wasn't hard to understand Nick's findings or believe his conclusion once you'd heard a couple of concrete examples. People were getting wise to their government being coopted by the filthy rich and ruthless business entities.

Not that this was anything new. But modern life had gotten so cluttered with information. Everything was getting so abstract, it was hard to follow a train of thought anymore. Phoebe hoped that now, when people could participate online in an instant virtual riot, maybe things would change.

#Democrazy would have a chance to become Democracy again.

"Unbelievable," Nick said, his voice hardly above a whisper.

His work was safe now. The whole world was safer now. Phoebe beamed and gave him a side hug.

What wasn't clear from any of the versions of the chase footage was exactly who the bad guys were or what had happened to them.

As usual Fox suggested it was liberal conspiracy, and the other networks speculated it was right-wingers who were under investigation by the FBI or NSA, but clearly no one knew for sure.

Phoebe decided it might be better not to know.

Leon, Ivy, and Phoebe speculated about whether or not the first couple of fellows they'd encountered had managed to find their way out of Sanderson's Hell. They suspected not. Phoebe imagined them in shredded jumpsuits, still crawling around in the dense briars, scratched and bleeding, swearing at each other.

When the excitement subsided, Doc cleaned and dressed Phoebe's and Fred's scratches and scrapes and closed a little cut on Nick's forehead with a butterfly band-aid. "You won't get any disfigurement from that," Doc said, "not at your age. It's one of the advantages of being older. Scars don't show."

Nick shot him a rueful look.

Phoebe's dear friend Waneeta arrived. Waneeta was real handful, a force of nature. She told Nick she was an *arthur*, too. After Appalachian Rural Healthcare had collapsed in the wake of healthcare reform she'd started writing to support herself. "I got way more books out there than you do, buddy."

Waneeta had gone straight to indie publishing, starting with e-book wedding guides. She was an expert at planning weddings. She'd been married four times, so far. Fortunately for her, the fourth husband was turning out to be a great guy.

She told Nick she'd been making a decent living from selling wedding guides, but now the big money was coming from what she referred to as her *lady porn*.

"She means them *smut* books," Jill said, laughing.

Phoebe disapproved of the explicit extremes of the romance genre, but knew it was lucrative and Waneeta needed the money. Her friend had an irrepressible spirit and Phoebe loved her no matter what.

Nick was grateful for the opportunity to encounter Leon and Ivy in less strained circumstances. They chatted and Nick thanked them sincerely for all their help. He explained where Leon's truck was, and Ivy said she'd drive Leon over to the chateau the next morning so he could retrieve his beloved vehicle.

The Gryphon stood gazing out onto Central Park from his eyrie. Billions of dollars and thousands of employees at his disposal and yet a handful of rednecks had thwarted him. Their stunning victory was being thrown in his face twenty-four hours a day via the news channels.

They had to have had help. The media storm was incredible.

That he'd been beaten on this scale by a people with no discernable resources was unimaginable. Unbelievable. Unbearable.

His world was collapsing. Social media was allowing all the little people to band together in great swarms, like gnats. Grassroots coups were taking place right and left. People around the world were actually threatening to take charge of their governments.

He kicked the heavy glass of the wall as hard as he could.

All he achieved was a scuffed shoe and sore foot.

He hoped it wasn't a metaphor for the rest of his life.

Even one of the rangers fighting wildfires in California became aware of Nick and Phoebe's adventure. Someone got in touch with Henry and gave him a heads up about Phoebe's shenanigans, probably Waneeta. He called the café and asked for Phoebe. Phoebe turned her back on the room to try to speak with at least a modicum of privacy.

"Girl, what's this I hear about you climbin curtains and stealin cars?" he said when Phoebe answered. "Can't leave you alone for a minute without you goin rogue."

She laughed and said, "Maybe you're not the only person in the world with fires to put out."

"That's true," he agreed. Then he asked how she was doing and they chitchatted amiably until she could hear men calling him in the background.

"You better go," she said. "Be careful. Come back safe."

"You, too," he said with emphasis, and hung up.

Men, thought Phoebe, for the millionth time. They were the only ones who were ever supposed to do anything interesting.

CHAPTER 35

It was now Tuesday morning and Phoebe showed up bright and early for her second day on the job. She brought Nick with her again, because he wanted to thank *Le Seigneur*.

They'd eaten at the café, watched some more of the apparently endless news footage of themselves, then gone to Leon's to retrieve Phoebe's Jeep. They'd spent the night at her modest farmhouse, both so exhausted they'd collapsed into separate rooms and been aware of nothing until Phoebe's alarm went off the next morning.

Now they were navigating the halls of the monastery, exchanging nods with various religious affiliates as they passed. "I know it sounds crazy," Nick whispered, "but these people all seem sort of ... familiar. It's like I know them, but I'm certain I've never met any of them before."

"Same here," Phoebe agreed, "It's weird."

While *Le Seigneur* and Nick talked, Phoebe reviewed her patient's orders and the doctor's notes and instructions about his care. She heard Nick make several mentions of the Chinese and there was a lot of complicated discussion of world trade policies as she inventoried and organized her boss's medicines and prepared his upcoming regime.

When they were finished, she checked *Le Seigneur's* vital signs, helped him take his pills, and measured out the doses of several plant tinctures that had been prescribed, such as *Angelica archangelica* and *Prunus spinosa*.

He seemed tired already, although it was only 10 o'clock in the morning. Phoebe wondered if he'd stayed up late or perhaps hadn't slept at all. She wanted to ask about the nature of his ailment, because it wasn't spelled out anywhere on any of the paperwork she'd seen, but before she could broach the topic, he spoke.

"You did a good thing, you know," he said, gifting her with his angelic smile. "You have several remarkable talents, in addition to your nursing skills. You could be quite useful around here, if you are interested in helping out."

"I'd be glad to help you any way I can," said Phoebe.

"You kept Nicolas safe. He was a total stranger, but circumstances thrust him into your care and you did an impressive job as his protector."

"We protected each other," Phoebe said.

"Even better. Then perhaps you will not mind escorting him to our friends in New York. He has achieved the sort of media saturation that I believe is termed *a mile wide and an inch deep*. At this point it is imperative for him to add substantive depth to his acrobatic acclaim."

Nick and Phoebe exchanged smiles.

"I need you to take him to the Frick mansion if you would. There is a relationship of longstanding between the St. Cloud and Frick families. The significance of the connection is not widely known, but you might find it interesting that the Fricks rented the St. Cloud's New York home in the early 1900s while their house was being built.

"You will be given assistance there. It is a ... safehouse. While you are there I suggest you take the opportunity to enjoy the architecture as well as the paintings. The building and the furnishing are quite wonderful. It's the finest collection of paintings in the world and a wonderfully pleasant home."

"Sure," Phoebe agreed, "It sounds fun."

Le Seigneur searched her face, then said, "As you may have surmised, a regular part of our work involves delivering certain people, and sometimes *objets*, here and there."

Phoebe nodded, although she had no earthly idea what kind of business he was in. She trusted her gut, though, and the goodness, even saintliness, that radiated from the man. And she needed a job, so she'd continue to play along, at least until she got a whiff of anything unseemly.

"I need a resourceful, trustworthy courier as urgently as I need a competent nurse. Getting both in one person is a blessing indeed," he said.

"After you deliver Nicolas, if you could courier an *objet d'art* for our friends at the Frick Collection, I would greatly appreciate it. We'll handle the travel arrangements, of course, from New York, after Nicolas is settled. It should be an interesting trip."

Phoebe looked at her patient with her eyebrows raised. She wasn't sure she was prepared for any further interesting experiences.

"This time, because you have become rather well known, we will provide special assistance with your security. We'll be sending Christophe St. James with you."

"Ah, here he is."

A tall unbelievably handsome man stepped into the doorway and gave Phoebe a formal half bow as a greeting. He was wearing blue jeans and a white t-shirt. He had gray eyes and a head of sun-streaked light blond hair that he wore loose. It fell to his waist in a thick, straight, totally gorgeous mass. Phoebe had never seen anything like it except on the covers of Viking romance novels. She got the odd feeling again—that she'd met the fellow somewhere before, but this time she was positive that she hadn't. He wasn't someone you could ever forget seeing.

After that brief introduction during which Christophe spoke not a single word, he left. Apparently none of the people who worked at the *School for Mysteries* engaged in small talk. Phoebe plumped up her boss's pillows and helped him recline comfortably. Then she tidied the bed and the table next to it.

She had the chance to look closely at the single piece of decoration in the room—the wonderful little painting of St. Michael and the Dragon that sat on the bedside table. What she saw on closer inspection made her gasp. The knight in the painting looked exactly like Christophe.

After work Phoebe let Nick drive her Jeep to the rendezvous point. Their transportation to New York was nothing like anything either of them had expected. It was a bus—a very large, very fancy tour bus with darkened windows and no identifying markings except for a Tennessee license plate. When they approached it, each carrying a bag containing the clothing and toiletries provided by Arabella, the doors opened and they were invited in by a slender man in worn blue jeans and a ragged t-shirt.

"Hi. I'm Billy," he said in a local East Tennessee accent. "Glad ye could join us."

It took Phoebe a few seconds and an awkward double take to realize that this was Billy Benson. He was the biggest country music star in the world. She tried not to stare or do anything weird, but she was sure it was obvious from her jerky body language that she'd recognized him. She realized it must be a pain to be constantly on the receiving end of goofy stares and tongue-tied people, or people who were doing what Phoebe was, trying to look anywhere but at him.

"We're headin to New York. I got a show tomorrow night," he said, "and we figured my tour bus was as safe a way as any to git ye there in one piece. Andy," he said, indicating the driver, "will git us there by mornin."

Phoebe looked down the hall toward the back of the bus. "Wow, this thing is *big*," she said.

"It's my dang house for half the year," Billy said. "There's three bedrooms. My stuff's in the one in the back, so ya'll can fight over who gets the one on the left and who gets the one on the right. They're pretty much identical."

"We got a kitchen, and a media room, and a couple of bathrooms with showers. Ye can make yerself somethin to eat, or hang out in yer rooms. Do whatever suits ye. I'm gonna sit up here with Andy for a while and see if I can git some work done."

Nick gave no indication that he'd recognized Billy, perhaps he didn't. "I'm exhausted," he said. "If it's all the same to you, I think I'll turn in now."

He made his way down the hall to the first empty room he came to and flung himself facedown on the bed. He went to sleep almost immediately.

Phoebe went back to the kitchen and rummaged through the refrigerator. She was making herself a cheese sandwich when she heard soft guitar playing and singing coming from the front of the bus. Billy had the sweetest voice.

She sat on a couch next to the kitchen table and before she could take even one bite of her sandwich, she slumped to one side, lulled into sleep by one of the best singers in the world.

CHAPTER 36

Neither Nick nor Phoebe stirred until Billy woke them on Wednesday morning. Somehow during the night Phoebe had gotten a pillow under her head and been covered with a quilt. Her cheese sandwich was on the kitchen table. The first thing she did after sitting up and wiping the slobber off the side of her face was take a big bite out of it. She was starving.

Billy said he'd woken them up in plenty of time to have hot showers, change clothes, and have some breakfast before they'd be dropped off in the City. Nick and Phoebe went their separate ways to do as he suggested. When they were cleaned up and changed they regrouped in the kitchen. Phoebe started back in on her cheese sandwich.

"I've never slept so well in my life," said Nick.

"Me either," Phoebe agreed. "It's like when you're a kid, sleeping in the car on vacation. Something about the road sounds and the movement."

She felt great. Nick was obviously feeling chipper, too. It was wonderful to see him happy. They'd only known each other for a few days, but he seemed to be changing drastically hour by hour. It was a good change.

A half hour later they said their goodbyes to Billy and Andy and got off the bus in the concealment of the covered service entrance to the Frick Collection.

They were met by a woman who was apparently the counterpart of Arabella Devlin-Forrest. She introduced herself as Isabella Borbón y Polo-Villaverde and said she would be assisting Prince de Mars with his intra-city travel arrangements.

She pronounced Prince with a French accent. It sounded like *prawnce*, to Phoebe. Phoebe wasn't crazy about the idea that Nick was a prince. She was even less thrilled with him being a *prawnce*.

When Isabella would have led Nick away, he said, "Can you give us a minute, please?"

The woman bowed and backed away. Phoebe didn't know if walking in reverse was something she did for everyone or if it was only for royalty. Either way it was goofy looking, but it would certainly help to minimize the opportunity for anyone to notice if you had a large rear end.

Focus, she told herself and turned toward Nick. He was looking at her with a wistful expression. She knew how he felt.

"If you're worried about the interviews," she said, "just remind yourself that one of your names is Fulk. With a name like that, you don't have to take any crap off anybody."

He smiled.

"I'm gonna miss you," Phoebe said.

"This isn't the last you'll see of me," he said.

"I know," she replied, "Your mug will be on every television news show and every form of media known to mankind for the next few days. They might even name a highway overpass after you."

He took both her hands and held them tight, then he hugged her for a long time.

Phoebe started crying. In two days they'd almost completely reversed roles. Now *she* didn't want to leave *him*.

Nick's back was to Isabella, but Phoebe could see the woman over his shoulder. She stood silently and waited a discreet distance away as they said their farewells. Phoebe suspected Isabella had seen a lot of emotional partings like this, considering her line of work, whatever it was—travel agent to people with hits out on them, perhaps.

Phoebe pulled herself away and stepped back, sniffing and wiping her face with her hand, "You've gotta go do your celebrity thing and I've gotta go be a secret agent."

"I know that your new friend Thor is taller than me, stronger, smarter, and a lot better looking, but at least I am a mortal man. It's pathetic, isn't it, that my best selling point is that I will one day, die."

Phoebe had to laugh.

"I mean, the guy never smiles, or even frowns. He's something.... weirdly spectacular. You don't wanna go there."

"Stop being silly, of course he's a regular person. What else could he be?"

"What I'm trying to say is, I know it's part of your nifty new job to go places with a man who makes Fabio look like a girl, but I'm just asking for you not to get involved with him right away. Don't get engaged before I get back. At least give me a chance. When I'm rich and famous, I promise I'm coming back to get you," Nick said. "So be ready to be swept off your feet by me in a couple of hours."

Phoebe snorted as she brushed at the beautiful gray suede jacket

Billy had given him. He looked great except for the black eye.

"I'm serious," he said. "In a few minutes I'll be meeting an agent and lawyer to sign what I'm told is an eight-figure book deal. Then we're making the rounds of the studios here in town, and I'll end up at some place where I'll give back-to-back interviews by satellite to foreign media. So, in half an hour I'll be rich, and then ninety minutes after that, I'll be famous."

Phoebe was laughing and crying at the same time as she struggled to neaten his disorderly curls.

"I know my hair isn't as good as his," he said grabbing her hands.

"Your hair is fine. I'm not crying over your hair."

"Why else could you be crying? You haven't even seen the place in Normandy yet. Our house was one of the only ones that looked better after D-Day. I'll show it to you. We can take sleeping bags and a bunch of packets of instant hot chocolate. You'll love it. It's right on the ocean so there's this continuous breeze wafting through, mainly because the windows don't have any glass in them. It's extremely refreshing because the wind comes straight off the North Sea at up to ninety miles an hour."

He made himself laugh with that and had to let go of her so he could hold his ribs. "Laughing still hurts," he said, wincing.

Nick reached for Phoebe again and gave her the world's sweetest kiss, then he rested his cheek against hers and sighed into her ear. He whispered, "Don't fall in love with the Elf King."

He stood holding her for a last few moments, then slowly peeled himself away with great effort, and walked away with his new handler.

CHAPTER 37

Phoebe stood bemused, watching him go. They'd only known each other for a few days, but what a whirlwind it had been. When she recovered herself, she went to find whatever it was she was supposed to courier to parts unknown. The Frick mansion took up a full city block on Fifth Avenue between 70th and 71st Streets. The layout and proportions were lovely. The place had a wonderfully serene feel. Phoebe immediately decided it was her favorite house in the world.

Her unqualified approval faltered, however when she was ushered up the set of curving limestone stairs that would take her to the private areas of the house. A massive pipe organ was displayed on the first landing. Phoebe shuddered and had a flashback to St. Cloud. Pipe organs gave her the creeps. What was it with rich people and pipe organs? Was it some kind of Flintstone version of a Bose radio?

The word *organ* seemed repulsive when applied to something outside of a living body. There was a subtle implication that it might be like a lampshade made of skin or a necklace made of teeth or ears. If a kidney was an internal organ, was this an *external* organ?

Again Phoebe had to remind herself to focus. She tore her eyes away from the organ and noticed that just as St. Cloud had been, this house was open to the public and was filled with tourists. There were security guards everywhere here, though. One was positioned at the bottom of the staircase. No one was allowed upstairs without permission.

Phoebe was directed to a private office on the second floor of the mansion where she met Naintara Jain, a beautiful young Indian woman, sitting behind an antique desk wearing a brilliant red sari with golden embroidery along the edges.

Naintara stood and introduced herself with a charming British accent. She explained that the object Phoebe was to courier had just completed the process of being cleaned and restored at the Cloisters facility. She said Phoebe would be able to retrieve it on her way to Teterboro Airport.

Then Naintara thanked her, and said, "As soon as you are ready, we have a car waiting to take you."

Phoebe couldn't bring herself to try to say *Le Seigneur* with her accent, so she said, "The Boss," as she'd decided to call him, "said I might be able to look at some paintings while I was here."

"Of course," Naintara said. She used her phone to summon the Chief Curator to give Phoebe a tour.

The Boss had been right. The Frick was the most amazing collection of art she'd ever seen in her life. There were no *also rans* in this place—no lesser works by renowned painters, or works that were obviously *from the studio of* the greats. These were prime specimens from the hand of the master himself, each one giving testimony to an artist at the zenith of his powers.

Phoebe loved the portraits best. There was a fabulous one of a Doge by Bellini, an extraordinary head and shoulders image of an unknown man by Hans Memling, two Titians, and three Vermeers.

There were four Whistlers—two were studies in blacks and two were in whites. There were half a dozen palpably holy, religious scenes painted over a thousand years ago by unknown monks.

In the dining room Thomas Cromwell faced Sir Thomas More. Their portraits were hung on the same wall, but on opposite sides of the fireplace. El Greco's astonishing St. Jerome hung between them, over the mantle. There were four Rembrandts—the *Polish Rider*, a self-portrait of the painter from mid-life, and two iconic portraits of other people whose beautifully lit faces and costumes shone out from a black background.

These people all looked familiar, too, but Phoebe knew it was because their faces had looked out at her from countless art books. Phoebe had minored in Art History. It made her feel dizzy to see so many singular originals inside one man's house.

She was deeply and unexpectedly affected by the portrait of Sir Thomas More by Hans Holbein. There was something so moving about the slight beard shadow and delicate facial blush that were so realistically depicted on the great man. Phoebe felt as if he was alive and right in front of her.

This was *The Man for All Seasons* for goodness sakes—her idea of the perfect boyfriend. Meeting Sir Thomas like this, unexpectedly, a man Phoebe had always admired and had romantic fantasies about, made her burst into tears again. It was all too much—the new job, Nick, St. Cloud, Billy Benson's tour bus, and now Sir Thomas More.

It was time to leave. She made her way back to the service entrance and found Christophe already there, waiting. *Good grief,* Phoebe said to herself, as she looked at him. He was at least 6'2", but when you got up close to him he seemed even bigger. He radiated … something. It wasn't anything aggressive or scary, it was more like intense determination. His stormy gray eyes stood out in vivid contrast to his dark eyebrows, dark eyelashes, and a tanned face.

And that hair…. a long, straight, silky looking mane of white blond mixed with golden blond. It blew Phoebe's mind that he wore it loose without any self-consciousness. He didn't fiddle with it. Anyone else would need a ponytail holder, but not him.

But the most remarkable thing about him wasn't that he was spectacular looking. It was that even taking into consideration his height, physique, male attire, and his dark brown beard stubble, he still managed to give off an androgynous vibe. She looked at his face and tried to guess his age, but wasn't able to come to any conclusions.

What she was sure of was the instant anyone, male or female, laid eyes on him, they would want to marry him. He neither smiled nor frowned. His beautiful mouth was in a straight line that indicated only calm neutrality.

"Wait here," he said. "I'll go get the car," He had a deep voice and he spoke with a lyrical accent Phoebe couldn't place. Phoebe noticed when he walked, his footsteps made no sound.

When he was out of sight, the female African American guard posted at the door said, without moving a muscle, "Mm, mmm, mmmmm."

Phoebe had to agree.

Christophe came back with a dark green BMW X7 SUV and they headed down Fifth Avenue. Phoebe openly gawked at the famous cityscape as he drove. She particularly liked the trees in Central Park.

She tried to keep track of where they were. They'd started out at East 70th Street. But they were in the 50s when she noticed he was glancing into the rear view mirror frequently. "Is someone following us?

"Yes," he said. He drove around the block, then zigzagged through traffic. Phoebe had no idea where they were going until they passed Rockefeller Center. Phoebe recognized the building from television. Phoebe knew this was a building where Nick had an appointment. Christophe was apparently seeing something he didn't approve of. He rolled his window down and openly stared at a Lincoln Navigator across the street. The windows were blacked out, so she couldn't see who was in it, but whoever it was, they pulled away from the curb and drove off.

Christophe waited at the curb for about five minutes until Nick was brought down and they watched from across the street as he and his Frick handler got into the back seat of an Escalade and were driven to their next appointment. Phoebe was happy to see that he looked to be in good spirits. He was coping with the open spaces and the television appearances with calm courage and poise. Perhaps he was a prince among men, … or Martians.

Christophe pulled away from the curb and maneuvered through the crowded streets, this time heading up Madison Avenue for a few blocks. Then he turned and drove over to Park, went about a block, and pulled to the curb, "Don't get out," he said. "No matter what happens. Stay in the car."

He jogged across the street, hopped up onto the sidewalk on the far side, and turned to face the luxury apartment building he'd left Phoebe sitting in front of. It was 740 Park Avenue. Christophe looked up, way up, then stood there, obviously focused on a particular window. He might as well have been carved of stone. The only thing that indicated he was human were the long pale blond tresses buffeted by the breeze.

CHAPTER 38

The Gryphon was at home and on the phone. He turned to gaze out the window. Something drew his glance to the sidewalk across the street where he saw a man standing, looking up at him. He should've been too high, too far away for anyone to be able see him, but this particularly silhouette was unmistakable, and worrisome. He was certain Christophe could see him.

He picked up a pair of high-powered binoculars he kept on the deep windowsill and scanned the sidewalk. When he focused the eyepiece he saw Christophe was speaking to him. It was easy to read his lips. He was saying, "Back off."

Not bloody likely, the man thought to himself. He continued to trade stares with Christophe fifteen stories below until he heard a strange creaking noise, like something was being put in a terrible strain. It was gradually getting louder. He stood behind thick bulletproof glass and continued to think the generally insolent thoughts of the super rich and super arrogant until a hairline crack appeared. Tiny fractures rapidly began propagating along the glass directly in front of his face until he could feel an air leak.

He picked up the phone and spoke into it. His minions staking out the offices of ABC, NBC, CBS, CNN, and Fox, immediately broke off their surveillance and left, as did the cars that had been following the BMW.

The crack in the window increased just enough to allow a hint of the winds from the concrete canyon to blow into the Gryphon's living room, ruffle his hair, and send the papers on his coffee table flying. Then Christophe crossed the street and got back into the car.

"What were you doing?" Phoebe asked.

"Just conveying my regards," Christophe replied.

"Are we running from someone?" she asked.

"No," Christophe said, "It's best not run from anything unless you absolutely have to. Beings with a lesser level of consciousness generally have a chase reflex and you wouldn't want to inadvertently stimulate it."

Christophe got on the Henry Hudson Parkway and gave Phoebe a view of New Jersey lining the bluffs across the Hudson River. She craned her neck and glanced up and to her right at the buildings lining Riverside Drive. It took only a few minutes to reach the Cloisters. Phoebe realized they were there when Christophe turned onto a cobblestone road that spiraled up toward a hodgepodge of old stone buildings dominated by an ancient square tower.

The Cloisters was where the Metropolitan Museum of Art housed their medieval art and artifacts. It was built from parts of several European abbeys that had been taken apart stone by stone, brought to New York, and reassembled on a high bluff overlooking the Hudson River. The complex appeared to be guarding New York from New Jersey. It looked like a real medieval building because it was, sort of.

Some of it was from France, some from Spain. A cloister and chapter house from one place, a chapel from somewhere else. Phoebe had never been there, but she knew it contained the priceless unicorn tapestries and two of the most exquisite books in the world—the *Les Belles Heures* made for the Duc de Berry and the *Book of Hours* made for Jeanne d'Evreux.

Phoebe had always wanted to see those books. She loved books.

"Don't kill him," the Gryphon said. "It's too late. Killing him now would only lend credence to his story and give the press more reasons to keep talking about him.

"Let's play the race card. That always works well. There's the obvious ironic connection between race and de Mars' work, but our people also have a sentimental affiliation with it. It worked perfectly for us even before political correctness was invented. It will serve us very well this time, too, I believe.

"Oh, and find out about this woman. Who the hell is she?"

He watched a computer screen that was displaying an image of Phoebe taken during the chase through St. Cloud. As he watched, a freeze frame screenshot was taken and the image was enhanced. A scan of databases began. In less than a minute a Tennessee driver's license popped up.

"Phoebe McFarland," he read from the license. "Let's keep an eye on her. She may have been drawn into this by accident, but if she ever pops up again, we might want to do something about her."

Christophe led Phoebe up the worn stone stairs into the Cloisters complex. It was a wonderful place. It seemed enchanted, to Phoebe.

How could it not? The unicorns were kept here. And her two favorite books.

They walked among the visitors but rather than buying tickets, a guard unhooked a red velvet rope and waved them through to an area that was off limits to the public, the administrative offices and the restoration studios.

Christophe moved silently through the halls and up a flight of stone stairs so worn by a thousand years of foot traffic that they sagged in the middle. He stopped outside a medieval wooden door and knocked. Phoebe heard a muffled, "Enter!"

He held the door open for Phoebe and indicated that she should precede him into the room. They must've been in the tower. The room was square, austere, and made entirely of stone. There was a single small window high above their heads that illuminated the space with a gentle diffuse light. A battered and stained wooden worktable filled the center of the room. It was covered with a jumble of small hand tools and containers of chemicals.

A man sat at the table wearing a lab coat, gloves, and a high-tech magnifying headlamp with two loupes. He was using what looked like a jeweler's tool on a small box.

Phoebe saw the little box pop open and the man said, "Ha!"

Then he set the box on the table, shoved the elaborate headgear up onto his forehead, and looked to see who'd come into his domain. "Christophe!" he shouted. Phoebe was charmed that the man had spoken three times, using only a single word. She suspected he might be an eccentric. She hoped so.

"Simon, I have brought a new courier to meet you. Please allow me to introduce Miss Phoebe McFarland of White Oak, Tennessee.

"Miss McFarland, this is Simon Plantagenet."

Christophe's faint accent had pronounced the name not exactly in English and not exactly in French, so it took a couple of seconds for Phoebe to process the sound and formulate an approximate spelling. Then she realized what it was and couldn't help making a quick jerk of surprise.

She tried to act normal and reached out to shake hands, saying, "Hello Mr. Plantagenet."

He didn't shake her hand. Instead he held up his gloved hands and said, "Graphite, machine oil, and anticorrosive agents."

Phoebe remembered reading somewhere that commoners weren't supposed to touch kings. That was why Queen Elizabeth wore gloves.

"Please call me Simon," he said. "Everyone does, when they're not calling me Simon Says."

Phoebe was beginning to get a feel for these people, who they were, and how they operated. She knew one of the French numbers sounded like *sez*. She couldn't remember which one it was, but she remembered some of their best antique furniture was called something that sounded like *Louie Sez*.

This guy's was probably Simon the Umpteenth of something. She had no desire to go into it, though, so she said nothing.

Simon chatted with Christophe, but Phoebe had no idea what they were talking about. Instead she was having an internal dialog where she introduced herself as Phoebe Toyota, or Phoebe Lichtenstein, or By the Grace of God Her Serene Highness Phoebe Holy Roman Empress of White Oak.

This is America! Phoebe thought. *Get with the program.* Titles of nobility were banned in the Constitution. Granted, these people tended to lowball their names, but still.

Christophe was putting a necklace on Phoebe before she realized what was happening. He was saying something about a *lavaliere* and assuring Simon that it would be delivered to École Mystère *straightaway*.

Phoebe frequently experienced difficulty focusing. This was yet another of those interludes where her life seemed to be passing before her eyes like a dream. The inside of her head sounded like this: École Mystère. That sounds like it might be in France. Something hanging around my neck is going to France. That means I must be going to France. *Straightaway*.

She looked up into Christophe's heartbreakingly beautiful, totally serene face and said, "Ahhhh….."

CHAPTER 39

Christophe bundled her back into the BMW. Phoebe, who was still stuck in Medieval Dreamworld, was thinking of the passenger seat as riding *pillion* on a *destrier*. She stopped when she realized she was projecting herself into the scene depicted in the painting on *Le Seigneur's* bedside table. She didn't really want to live life as it appeared in religious paintings or on the covers of romance novels. Phoebe used to love to read romance novels when she was young, before she'd spent much time with actual men.

They headed for Teterboro airport. Phoebe marveled at her new life. It was impossible to take in the recent events. She counted off the days on her fingers, Sunday, Monday, Tuesday, and it was now Wednesday morning. It had been just three days, but now everything was different. Instead of being old and facing starvation and boredom, she now had a life that she actually looked forward to. And a new job that was interesting. She couldn't remember if she'd been told what it paid, but she wasn't worried about it. Her standard of living had improved beyond all recognition.

What a way to travel. It was fabulous. You didn't have to make any arrangements. You hardly needed luggage. Even the Queen of England had to carry a pocketbook, but Phoebe didn't! What could be better?

Everything was provided for you—money, food, clothes, transportation, accommodations, interesting sights, and destinations. She sighed in happiness just as the BMW went across the tarmac, and rolled right up to a splendid small jet before stopping. Phoebe hopped out and at the same time the door on the jet opened and a set of stairs deployed.

Christophe went first and then turned to encourage Phoebe to join him on board. The interior of the plane was beautiful, of course. It looked more like living room than an airplane. There were several big comfy chairs, a couple of tables, and even a couch!

"You may sit wherever you like," Christophe said, then he went toward the cockpit and stooped to speak to the uniformed pilot and co-pilot.

Phoebe sat in one of the heavily padded camel-colored leather chairs and closed her eyes and tried to relax. She imagined herself on the beach in the south of France. She pretended to be lazing in her private cabana, diaphanous white curtains fluttering around her, while the sound of surf lulled her to sleep.

Phoebe opened her eyes to find Christophe standing over her.

"There are things you need to know," he said. "So I must take this opportunity to speak to you now. You will be able to sleep later."

Phoebe wondered how much later. Did he mean later today or next week? But she didn't say anything. Instead she swallowed and tried to sit up straight. She hoped she hadn't been snoring. Or drooling.

"We believed you and Nicolas would be able to travel to New

York without being noticed, but we were wrong," he said. "Nicolas' emergence has drawn substantially more media attention than we anticipated, thanks to your exertions at *san clu*. It took a moment for Phoebe to realize he was saying St. Cloud with a French accent. She did a mental triple take from *san clu* to *sans* clue and then smiled at her own joke. It was perfect, *sans* clue, meaning *without a clue*. Yep, that said it all.

Christophe was still talking though and she'd missed some of what he was saying, "… has provoked the oppositional forces into a frenzy. They are redoubling their efforts to silence him and now they have added you to their watch list."

Phoebe nodded as if she was listening, but she wasn't. She still wore a goofy smile over her *sans* clue joke. It was a *bon mot* she told herself, impressed with her French.

"This flight will take about six and a half hours, so there is plenty of time to talk," Christophe said. He gave her what she suspected was his version of a smile, but it came from his eyes rather than his mouth, which stayed set, as ever, in a fabulicious-looking straight line.

"I do not want to bore you, but I am not sure how much *Le Seigneur* told you," Christophe said," and I am not sure how much you have come to understand on your own. We certainly did not expect to run into you this time around. You arrived as his nurse, did you not?"

As usual Phoebe could follow only about half of what he was saying, but she nodded, "You mean the *Archangel?*"

"No, I mean your employer, your patient."

"I thought he was the *Archangel*?"

Christophe smiled with his eyes again, and said, "No, that would be me."

"Oh! Sorry. This mystery stuff is all so….."

"Mysterious?" he suggested, stone-faced.

"Exactly!"

"The word mystery, comes, in part, from the Greek word *mysterion*. There are actually two root words. One them translates as *with closed eyes* and another as *one who is initiated*."

"Which one am I?" Phoebe asked.

"That remains to be determined. Perhaps this would be easier if you asked me what you would you like to know."

"What do you mean when you say you didn't expect to run into me? The boss, my patient, *Le Seigneur*, said something like that, too. He said he expected Nick, but not me. Why would either of you expect either of us?"

"Do you understand about reincarnation?" he asked.

Phoebe shook her head slowly. "I understand some of the basics, but I don't believe in it. I'm a Christian."

"You realize that more than half the world believes in it, that it has always been part of the religious belief of most of the people on earth? And that more than half the people in the Christian world, when pressed, will admit to believing that it might be possible?"

Phoebe hadn't really thought about it before.

"It is touched on in several places in the Bible. The reality of reincarnation used to be common knowledge, but long ago the Catholic bureaucracy suppressed all of the writings about it because it was easier to gain control of people if they believed they had only one lifetime and that only through the priests could they aspire to heaven."

Phoebe wasn't prepared to jump on board with this yet.

"Well, it does not matter if you believe in it or not, it is a fact. One lifetime is not sufficient for anyone to experience enough, learn enough, or become wise enough to develop into a fully realized, selfless, force for good."

That made sense, but Phoebe was still reserving judgment.

"A facet of reincarnation is a tendency for clusters of individuals to reincarnate over and over in a certain proximity to each other. The nature of the relationship will change from parent, to sibling, to friend, to co-worker, but certain people will recur in our lives. That is why people who have never met before in this life will sometimes be able to make friends immediately, for no apparent reason. Or the opposite, people will take an instant, violent dislike to each other for no ostensible reason.

"Part of our task in each lifetime is to learn to notice these reactions and balance them out, to consciously work out our karma with other people. You are familiar with the term karma?"

Phoebe nodded.

"In between the time after we die and when we are born again, we make plans to accomplish certain objectives in our next life for the development of our spirit. We agree to work with certain other people on this or that project. People are able to consciously recall these pre-birth agreements, to a greater or lesser extent. Many people can at least sense them.

"If you are one of the sensitive ones, a so-called *psychic*, you can recognize these people when they arrive in your life. It saves a lot of time and trouble if you are able to remember what your task is and who your teammates are.

"On the odd occasion, like an unexpected emergency, the last minute substitution of a new teammate will be required. For example if one of the original team has been injured, or become sick or died unexpectedly, or has utterly forgotten their task—then the spiritual world, God or his angels, will send in a substitute to help. You, obviously, are one of these sorts of individuals."

Obviously? Phoebe pondered the idea. She wanted to reject it out of hand. She would've been terrified to learn what sort of thinking was going on inside the brains of the maniacs she'd been hanging around with if they weren't all so darn high-functioning. And interesting. And fun. And gorgeous. And if she and Nick hadn't both commented on how eerily familiar some of the strangers seemed who were suddenly popping up in their lives.

"I think I'm gettin a headache," she said.

"That is understandable. This is a lot to take in, all at once."

And they hadn't even gotten to the part about what her task might be, or what the need to courier people and objects was all about, or who the people were who were chasing her and Nick.

"If you're gonna keep talkin, I'm gonna need a cheese sandwich," Phoebe said. "You got any cheese on this plane? And bread? Preferably toasted. And I'm gonna need Diet Coke, lots of Diet Coke."

"I'm sure we can arrange something," Christophe said. He stood, offering his hand to help her up.

Only then did Phoebe realize they'd taken off. She looked out the window and saw they were flying over the ocean. Wow. No flight attendant had lectured them. Neither of them had fastened a seatbelt. There didn't seem to be anyone else on board aside from the two of them and the two pilots.

Phoebe sighed. Such was her new life. She took Christophe's warm hand, heaved herself out of the comfy chair, and followed him to the galley. She was hungry.

CHAPTER 40

Once she'd had her cheese sandwich on toasted sourdough, a big glass of milk, and two Chips Ahoy chocolate chip cookies, she felt ready to continue her tutorial from the *Archangel*. She'd been very reluctant to believe in all this wacky talk until she discovered that the jet was stocked with whole milk and a full size bag of Chips Ahoy cookies.

That had done more than anything else to convince her that there really was magic in this world. Clearly angelic forces beyond her understanding were at work and they were on her side. She wiped crumbs from her face and watched Christophe read from a tablet. *He's as beautiful as an angel*, Phoebe thought.

"Thank you," he said, without looking up.

She didn't realize she'd spoken out loud. In fact, she didn't think she had. She blushed at having been caught looking at him. Now that she was already humiliated, she couldn't resist asking him what she really wanted to know, "What's it like to be perfect looking?"

Phoebe wasn't ugly, but she wasn't a real looker either. People always complimented her on things like her sense of humor or her brains. All her life she'd wondered what she might've been able to achieve if she'd been beautiful, too.

"It's fantastic," he said, still surfing the net with his tablet. "I can have everything my heart desires without the slightest effort. People line up to give me anything I could possibly want before I can even think to ask for it. It can get annoying, but it is also wonderfully handy."

She had to smile at his candor.

"Our looks, our brains, every aspect of our lives is a test of character. What we do with what we have, that is the big question. But, when we get a chance, I will take you to my stylist. You can do a *lot* more with what you have. You will be surprised. Hair first, then clothes."

Oh, he's gay, she thought.

"Nope," he said.

That time she was certain she hadn't actually spoken out loud.

She got another cookie and said, "The Boss, *Le Seigneur*, said some stuff to me and Nick about a *School for Mysteries*. What did he mean?"

Christophe turned off his tablet and set it aside. Apparently this question was pleasing to him. "The purpose of the cosmos is to evolve," he said, "to increase consciousness, to become free, and then to use that freedom selflessly for the benefit of others. It is a big job, a huge, long-term effort.

"There have always been people who were more advanced in their understanding, more aware of things, and thus more capable of actively participating in the evolution of consciousness. The saying that it is lonely at the top is even more apropos at the highest levels of human consciousness. Recall that the finest specimens of humanity fell asleep at the Garden of Gethsemane.

Only the men, thought Phoebe.

"You are correct of course and that is a very advance and meaningful observation," said Christophe. "So these awakened people naturally tended to seek each other out. They tried to congregate and form schools so the more advanced individuals could teach the pupils who had the greatest potential.

"During all the ages these schools are known to have existed. Although their teachings were held in the strictest secrecy, the existence of the schools themselves was not always a secret. Some of the schools and their teachers were quite famous, for example, Zarathustra, and some of them less so, like Alanus ab Insulus, or as his name is said in French instead of Latin, Alain de Lille. He was teacher at Chartres, which was the last of the great mystery schools."

"Was Buddha one of the teachers?"

"Yes," he said. "The mystery schools have been in many places around the world at different times. The most well-known ones were, in chronological order, in India, Persia, Egypt, Greece, Ireland, and France."

"Does this have something to do with why we are going to France?"

"Yes."

Phoebe waited for him to say more, but he didn't. That, in itself, seemed ominous. He wasn't afraid to talk to her about reincarnation, karma, and the schools for mysteries, but whatever was coming, he didn't want to talk about. Phoebe excused herself and went to get some more milk.

The galley was next to the cockpit and the door was standing open. Phoebe peeked in. The pilot sensed someone behind him and glanced over his shoulder. "You're welcome to come in if you'd like," he said.

She crept forward into the small space that was crammed with electronics. The dashboard was massive and wrapped around. There were dozens, probably hundreds, of switches. How could anyone ever learn what they were all for? Just thinking about it made her dizzy.

"What kind of plane is this?" Phoebe asked.

"It's a Gulfstream G550 V9," the co-pilot said.

"How fast are we going?"

He glanced at a gauge and said, "476 knots. That's about 550 miles an hour."

"How high up are we?"

"Our current altitude is 47,000 feet."

Phoebe was startled. She had no idea what number she'd expected to hear, but that sounded really high, like a space ship. She tried to cipher it out in the head and said, "That's almost nine miles!"

She leaned forward to peer out. "The window feels cold."

"It's about -70° out there."

"*Minus* seventy?"

There was nothing but water below them. No signs of solid ground whatsoever, and a lot of sky. "Where are we?"

"The middle of the Atlantic Ocean," the co-pilot said. "It's about 3,600 miles from New York to Paris. But don't worry. This is a heavy jet, it has a lot of range. We don't need to hug the coast. The smaller jets have to do that because they need to stay over land as much as possible. They don't have enough fuel to make it straight across like we do, so they fly in an arc over Canada, Iceland, and Ireland."

She looked at the dark blue ocean, then thanked the two men and went back to her seat. Christophe had moved to the back, so apparently class was dismissed. Phoebe flopped down onto the couch, sagged over onto her side, and promptly fell asleep.

CHAPTER 41

By the time Phoebe woke up they'd flown from daylight into the darkness. Phoebe tried to remember what day it was. It had been Wednesday when she went to sleep, but during the night it must've become Thursday. Christophe said they were getting close to France. Phoebe kept an eye out for anything she could recognize. She knew Chartres was near Paris and to the southwest of the great city, but she didn't know if they were headed to some special landing strip there, or if they'd have to continue on to Paris to land and then double back by car or train.

She squinted into the darkness and made out a narrow band of glowing white on the horizon. She decided it might be the west coast of France. Within moments the plane flashed over clusters of light that must've been villages and towns but she couldn't discern anything in particular as they zoomed toward the center of France.

It was still dark when they landed at a private airport outside Chartres. They were met by a young man who introduced himself as Phillipe. He took some paperwork from Christophe and carried it to an immigration official. Phoebe watched an animated discussion. There was a great deal of gesturing. It dawned on Phoebe that she'd arrived without a passport. After a few minutes of extremely lively debate, and much shrugging, Christophe and Phoebe were whisked away by Phillipe in his small white Peugeot.

"He is my wife's cousin," said Phillipe nodding toward the immigration officer, as if that explained everything. He drove them at astonishing speed along narrow, but well-maintained paved roads and into the city of Chartres. The streets became progressively more narrow. The most slender of them was little more than alley and was paved with bumpy cobblestones. Phillipe whipped into a parking space next to an elegant building faced with ashlar limestone typical of 18th century France.

He hopped out and opened Phoebe's door for her before she could do it herself. "Madame," he said, with a flourish. Phoebe was a little disappointed that they would be transacting their business, whatever it might be, in a regular building rather than the Cathedral, but she kept a lid on it.

A few minutes later she was glad she hadn't spoken because they *were* headed for the Cathedral. The structures in the center of the city were built so tightly together it was hard to see that they were actually next to the Cathedral. She noticed this when it occurred to her to look up instead of horizontally.

Girl, you're not in White Oak any more, she said to herself, as she took in the massive spires and flying buttresses.

There was an odd density to the air. It increased as they walked along the cobblestone streets, heading for the Cathedral. Like other well-known power spots like the Smokies or Sedona, there was a palpable difference in the vibes. It was becoming overpowering. They were approaching a holy place. Phoebe was afraid she was going to cry.

They came out of an alley and into the open space surrounding the Cathedral and she could see it. She hadn't really known what to expect, but something about this wasn't right. She had no idea why she believed this, but she was certain of it.

Phillipe and Christophe continued up the walkway and headed to the nearest entrance, but Phoebe balked, confused. She felt rooted to the spot and couldn't make herself go any further.

Christophe came back to where she was standing and looked at her. "Are you having memories?" he asked gently.

Tears began to stream down her face. "This place…it's not right." She was feeling extremely disoriented, like she was losing her mind. She swiped at her eyes and said, "I don't even know what I'm sayin."

Christophe stepped close to her and put his arm around her. "Just let it come. You are remembering. It is normal. It is good."

"People *died* here," she said, grief stricken. "They killed the monks here, didn't they? And there was a fire. But not at this place," she said, pointing at the Cathedral. "It didn't look like this. It was over there," she pointed to one side of the Church, to an area of lawn that now stood empty. "The good place was over there, not here. But I don't know what it was."

She wiped her face with her hands and sniffed, calming down now that the initial shock was over. "Can we go over there?" she asked.

Christophe nodded. He walked her slowly over to the patch of lawn that seemed important to her in a way she couldn't understand. She stood there, utterly overwhelmed, a flood of tears silently streaming down her face. "I'm sorry," she said, sniffing. "I know I'm being crazy."

"Not crazy," Christophe said, "You are standing on the site of *The School of Chartres*. It was here long before this Cathedral. You are standing on the place that was the center of Christendom for hundreds of years. But at the end of the 13th century, the school was attacked, the students were killed, and the building was burned, then razed.

"It is not permitted for me to say anything about your particular incarnations, but I can tell you we are also standing on a ley line. You are feeling that, I think, as well. There is a line that extends across Europe that runs through many holy sites. Some people can feel it, some can't. We brought you here to see if you would remember. We thought it would help and we knew it would be easier for you from now on if you could. Now that you have been shocked like this, you will begin to awaken and sense your destiny, and remember your task for this lifetime."

Phoebe stood leaning against Christophe and wailed, "They killed the teachers."

"Yes," Christophe said. "The very last of the holy men who had actual experience of the oneness of all things. The last of the ones who were capable of active contact with the spiritual world. But it was alright. They knew this change had to come and they were prepared for it.

"It was necessary for the world and men to go dark, all the way, so we could then learn to make our way back to God using our own consciousness. No more passive mysticism, no more intercession through priests, no more throwing ourselves at the feet of Christ and asking to be saved without any work on our own behalf. Those days had to end.

"Christ needs co-workers now, He needs for us to work beside Him as His brothers. And He is taking a terrible gamble to see if we will be able to step up to the mark. Romans 8:22 *For we know that the whole creation groaneth and travaileth in pain together until now.*

"This is the only way for us to develop free will. That is our job—to reestablish our connection to Heaven through our own efforts on an individual basis.

"Because the angels do not have free will, they have never been tested in this way. They do not fully understand what it is like for us to be down here with a limited consciousness and exposure to evil. We are doing something the angels have the greatest respect for. And they need for us to succeed. Heaven is relying on us."

CHAPTER 42

"All of creation is relying on us. It is up to us to chose to love, to be selfless, even to people outside our own families, even to our enemies, even though nearly everything in our conscious mind and this material world is telling us that that is a mistake."

"I'm scared," Phoebe said.

Christophe hugged her hard. "Who wouldn't be? The future of the entire Cosmos is riding on it. But you had to wake up first. And now you have. That is something important. Now there is one more awakened human being on the right side of things. That is the way we have to do it now. One soul at a time."

She could feel herself drawing strength from him, even though as he held her so tightly she could also sense for the first time how exhausted he was. He was tired beyond imagining, but it hadn't diminished his beauty.

"You will become more conscious about things now. You will gradually learn to discern where your consciousness is residing. You will learn to be more objective rather than whimsical and subjective, not only about the small things, but even about your own existence.

"The biological mechanism of the body wants to live. That is all it knows. But the spirit knows better. It does not experience fear or death. The soul feels emotions, and mediates between our life body and our spirit. Our soul feels fear and greed and grief. But our spirit has direct knowledge and experience that it is eternal. We have to learn to maintain conscious contact with our spirit or we cannot function at a high level. This path is not for the weak ones."

They stood together, clinging to each other, until Phoebe felt capable of turning around and facing the Cathedral. She watched all the visitors milling around, taking pictures, oblivious to the great dramas that had played out between God and the Devil on the humble patch of lawn a few yards away. And to the implications of those great dramas.

"When you saved Nicolas, we realized you had been sent to us. Even though you were largely unconscious, you stepped up and improvised an effective solution and did what had to be done. That is a priceless quality. Indeed, look at the information that is flooding the global consciousness of humanity because of what you have done in the last few days!

"Those of us who work with *Le Seigneur* try to locate as many of our brethren as we can, as quickly as we can. And then we do whatever it takes to jump start their memories of their previous preparation."

"Like transporting me 4,500 miles and standing me on a patch of grass to see what, if anything, would happen?"

"Exactly," he said.

"What about this necklace," Phoebe asked, touching the chain around her neck. "Was that just a trick?"

"No, not a trick. We do need to deliver the lavaliere to an associate here. And we do not send these sorts of things in the mail. Miss McFarland, the sacred and the profane are always entwined. It is always a mixed bag, whoever you are dealing with and whatever you are trying to achieve. That is the fundamental nature of life on Earth."

Phillipe was waiting for them at an astonishing triple doorway surrounded by hundreds of statues carved into the exterior wall. He was spring-loaded to give Phoebe a tour of the Cathedral. They walked up the wide stone steps to the doors. The place was massive. And *cold* and *dark* inside.

"This is the first great gothic cathedral built in the world," said Phillipe. "It was built in a single great burst and has remained the most unchanged, the most intact, of all the great cathedrals.

"This building was mostly constructed between 1194 and 1250. A mighty impulse went out from this place. Chartres is the mother cathedral of Ameins, Reims, Rouen, Paris, Lincoln and Salisbury, Bamburg and Cologne."

It seemed ancient beyond the thousand years of the stone structure. It felt, and smelled, incalculably old. Phoebe decided to test her fledgling confidence in seat-of-the-pants notions. "There's something strong underneath here isn't there?"

Phillipe gave a tiny leap of excitement at the chance to tell her about the crypt beneath the church and the cult of the Black Madonna. "There is a healing well inside the cathedral that was in constant use until the French Revolution when it was desecrated. The Black Madonna was also destroyed during the Revolution.

"This place was a shrine to the eternal feminine. The founding relic of Chartres is not a dead body or a piece of a dead body like most other cathedrals. It is a veil said to have been worn by Mary during the birth of Jesus. There are no dead interred in this place— not a single grave, or tomb, or crypt.

"That is because this is a shrine to birth, not death. It is a place that celebrates the task of each human being to develop their consciousness so that they are able to have a direct experience of the divine. This is not a place of abstract scholarship or dull rote beliefs."

He jabbered as he led them to one of the enormous stone pillars that held up the roof. There was a gothic door in the base of the column. Phillipe touched three protuberances on a bit of stone carving beside the door in a sequence and there was a soft click. He opened the door and led the way up a tight spiral staircase. Christophe brought up the rear and closed the door behind them.

They climbed until Phoebe had to ask for a rest. She looked up as she waited to catch her breath. The staircase seemed to go on *forever*. She noticed Phillipe didn't bother to say, *It's not far now* or *We're almost there.*

She nodded when she was ready to resume the climb. Eventually they reached a landing and Phillipe opened another ancient looking wooden gothic door and led them into a small cluttered room. A beautiful, chic, silver haired woman was sitting behind a desk, wearing a nubby tweed Chanel suit and pearls. Phillipe introduced them. It was Chantelle.

She enquired about their trip. Phoebe was too out of breath to answer, so Christophe did it for her as he unfastened the clasp on her necklace and handed it over. Chantelle obviously knew and adored Christophe. Who wouldn't? They had an intense discussion about restaurants and Chantelle recommended one for lunch and a different one for dinner.

Christophe asked if Armand was around. She said he was. Then he spoke a couple of very fast sentences to her in French. Phoebe noticed this immediately because he'd never done it before.

She realized he was intentionally concealing something from her and said, "Would it help if I moved back so you two could conspire in private?"

He shook his head, "Not necessary."

Phoebe, Phillipe, and Christophe stood above the North Rose Window on an exterior walkway. They looked out across the city from their open-air perch. The dawn and the breeze were refreshing after the dark, still interior of the ancient building.

"I know your tour of St. Cloud was lacking in certain respects," Christophe said. "Would you like to see more of Chartres before we leave? Phillipe is a wonderful guide."

"Oh, yes, I'd love to," said Phoebe.

"If you decide to stay with us, you will have the opportunity to visit the other installations."

"Where are they?"

"All over the world," said Christophe. "Any person of modest intelligence with access to the internet can surmise where most of them are: Eleusis, Troy, Delphi, Rome, and Jerusalem. We use Essene, Templar, and Cathar sites, as well as Greek and Roman temples and cathedrals and monasteries. We have secular sites in chateaux and castles."

"Why don't the … bad guys … destroy your places?"

"Oh they do!" said Phillipe. "In fact, this cathedral is a good example. It has been burned down thirteen times that we know of, three major, ten minor. But we keep building it back. The first Goetheanum in Switzerland was burned to the ground in 1920. One of our people, Dr. Rudolf Steiner, invented reinforced concrete so we could build that one back and not have to worry as much about arson.

"They would love to annihilate our infrastructure," said Christophe, "but there would be … repercussions they are not prepared to deal with. They are in no position to conduct an overt war. For over two thousand years they have been confined to lying, harassment, vandalism, and the odd skirmish here and there. There are a lot of us and our people are quite resourceful and resilient, as you yourself demonstrated.

"Most of their modern attacks are in the realm of misinformation or disinformation campaigns, like the one Nick is exposing about the cause of war. They also produce a lot of fractured or deviant so-called esoteric scholarship, like most of the books and films about the Templars. The jewel in their crown would be *The Da Vinci Code*. It was a superbly paced work, highly entertaining, massively successful, but substantively it was absolute trash.

"You would think the man would be ashamed to say such things about Christ. If he's not sorry yet, he will be. That is the meaning of karma. If there's one thing that you can be certain of, everyone one of us will get exactly what is coming to us.

"But, as of yet, people don't realize this, so marketing a selfless lifestyle is difficult. It always has been. The concepts of esoteric Christian scholarship are not as conducive to sound bites as statements like the Da Vinci Code's: *Jesus had a baby!*

"That is something we are working with now. Our people tend to be scholars. It has been difficult to wean them off obscure tomes in dead languages and onto Twitter. It is understandable when you realize that our media people generally spent their previous incarnation in a medieval scriptorium. We are conceptually prying the quill pens and paintbrushes from their hands and giving them a smart phone.

"I believe you met Xander at St. Cloud. He refers to his task as *monk marketing*. It is a work in progress. Most of us in this movement who are incarnated now were monks in our last life. That is why so many of us never marry in this life. We are souls who have developed beyond normal social conventions and we are unconsciously honoring half-remembered vows of celibacy and poverty. Many of us were soldiers as well—Templars. It is why there is so much interest in the Templars these days. They were very important individuals in medieval times and many people have wisps of memories of them from former lives."

Phoebe wasn't sure how much she believed of what Christophe was saying, but she loved hearing him talk this way. It was simultaneously comforting and freeing to think that there was an honorable order and structure to life that she hadn't been aware of.

CHAPTER 43

Phillipe guided them around the cathedral, weaving inside and out on walkways high above the main floor. "This site was discovered 3,000 years ago—1,000 years before Christ, by Druids from what the Romans called Hibernia, but which is now called Ireland.

"It sits on a great limestone plain. The name Chartres comes from Celtic word *cairn* which means *place of the altar.* The Druids stayed here for 1,000 years.

"When Julius Caesar was conquering Gaul he reported a strong tribe of Celts here," Phillipe said. "Their Druid priests established a cult here devoted to the Black Madonna. And they defied the Romans. Shortly after the death of Jesus Christ, Joseph of Arimethea brought a small group of early Christians here, along with the Holy Grail, and they dedicated the site to the Virgin Mary."

Phoebe followed the men through the narrow stone passages that ran above or ducked underneath the flying buttresses. Christophe stopped and touched a simple carving on the wall, "Here is an autograph left by one of the early masons."

It was a star. Phoebe tried to picture a man tapping it out with a chisel and a heavy hammer, hoping to leave his mark for people to see a thousand years later. Christophe and Phillipe stopped a few more times and touched other similar signatures in stone like a triangle or a cross.

Something about the way Christophe touched the cross made Phoebe ask, "Did you know him?"

He looked at her and smiled with his eyes.

"Various sects convened here from the east and west," Phillipe said, "and then for 200 years, from 1000 to 1203, this was the home of the greatest school in Christendom. It was an increasingly heretical school that taught a Christianity based not on rote belief or passive faith, but on direct personal *experience* of Christ and the spiritual world that was attained through a meditative practice."

They went into the cavernous attic space that was above the vaulted ceiling, but underneath the roof. They walked along the boards that had been laid across rafters so they wouldn't be standing on the ceiling itself. It was amazing. Shafts of light came in through small trefoil windows spaced at regular intervals.

Phillipe led them down a tight spiral stone staircase to a walkway with long balconies that overlooked the interior. They were much lower now, but still quite high above the main floor.

"We're standing on the Triforium," Phillipe said. "The triforia in pagan temples were used for conversation or business. In the Christian basilicas they were usually reserved for women."

Phoebe looked around this mezzanine level of the cathedral. *Another freakin pipe organ*, she noticed. She was getting pipe organ PTSD. They were like a gigantic nightmare version of an accordion or a boombox for dinosaurs. "This is my third pipe organ in four days. They freak me out."

Phillipe shrugged and exchanged a look with Christophe.

As the three of them stood there, side-by-side on the high

balcony, a choir filed into the choir stalls down below and began to sing the most beautiful song Phoebe had ever heard in her life. "What are they singing?" she asked.

"It is an old arrangement of a Matins prayer *O Magnum Mysterium.* They are singing in Latin, 'O great mystery....'" said Phillipe.

Magnum Mysterium, and a *School for Mysteries,* Phoebe thought to herself. Her whole life was one big mystery these days. Phillipe led them down to the main level. They walked in silence, surrounded by the unearthly beauty of the choir singing the heartbreakingly gorgeous prayer.

"Most holy sites were built with an east to west axis that coincided with the rising and setting of the sun," said Phillipe. "All except for Chartres. Here the central nave is canted to the northeast so rays from the sun fall on the altar and light up the central axis of cathedral on the midsummer solstice."

Phillipe checked his watch. He'd done that several times during their tour. He led them to the center of the nave. Christophe stood behind her and put a hand on each of her shoulders as if to steady her.

As the choir sang about great mysteries, the miracle of the building unfolded in front of her—the sun began to pierce the gloom of the interior. Phoebe watched the light move as the sun rose.

"Today is the summer solstice," Christophe said.

Phoebe looked at him over her shoulder. There were tears in her eyes.

"This is a gift to you from *Le Seigneur*. It is our thanks for saving Nicolas."

They stood for several minutes watching the sun perform its magic illuminating the interior of the cathedral.

"If you look down at your feet you will see that we are standing atop a famous labyrinth."

Phoebe did as she was told and noticed the large maze delineated by the different colors of stone in the floor.

"Many structures are aligned with rising or setting sun on the summer or winter solstice, or spring or fall equinox," Phillipe said. "Chartres is created to capture the light from the summer solstice. In the ancient Essene community where the Dead Sea Scrolls were found, the largest room of the communal building at Qumran is aligned with the summer solstice. So is Stonehenge.

"Newgrange in Ireland is aligned to the winter solstice. The Parthenon, and the copy of it in Nashville, is aligned with the winter solstice."

Phoebe looked around at the amazing colors of the stained glass. "These windows are fabulous."

"There are almost two hundred of them," Phillipe said. "They were saved from damage during World War II by a few dozen elderly local people who removed all of them and hid them in just five days."

Phoebe's rapture was crushed when she heard something she hadn't anticipated. It was the muted, but unmistakable screeching and groaning of the ultimate buzz kill. "Please tell me they're not about to fire up that pipe organ."

Phillipe was smiling, but Christophe maintained his inscrutable calm poise. The opening notes of the tune were not what she expected. It wasn't Bach. It was The Who. "Holy moly. That's *Baba O'Reilly*!" Phoebe said.

Then she remembered Christophe asking about someone named Armand and the rapid French he'd spoken to Chantelle. "Is that Armand?"

"Oui." Christophe said.

"This is great!"

"*Exactement.*"

"Why not *Stairway to Heaven*?"

"He has done that one before and gotten into trouble," said Phillipe, "so he dare not do it again. He may get into difficulty for this, also, but Christophe assured us you had earned it."

It was about noon on the longest day of the year. Phoebe already felt like it was the longest day in her whole life and they were barely half way through it. "Would you like to have lunch?" Christophe asked.

They strolled through the streets to the restaurant Chantelle had recommended. Phoebe's body clock was totally messed up. Her sleep and her meal times had been wildly disrupted. She guessed it was early morning in White Oak, but wasn't sure.

The meal was fabulous of course. They sat at the outdoor café for a couple of hours. Phillipe, Christophe, and the waiter debated every aspect of the feast in great detail. She had to admit she felt a lot better afterwards. Finally Christophe searched her face and asked, "Are you ready for your encounter with *haute couture*?"

Phoebe drew a deep breath and nodded.

"You will be astounded at what half a day in Paris can do for you."

He was right.

CHAPTER 44

It was amazing to experience life as it existed for Christophe. Wherever he went the cosmos seemed to stop whatever it had been doing for the previous eons so it could revolve around him instead. And the massive displays of cheek kissing were beyond comical to Phoebe.

The first stop was at a hair salon. "The colorist here is a genius," said Christophe.

"I didn't realize you colored your hair," Phoebe said, "It looks so natural."

"Of course it looks natural! It *is* natural. I meant the colorist here has the skill to do highlights that actually match my hair. All the women want this color. Many try, but very few can achieve it."

Christophe supervised the famous stylist as he worked on Phoebe. The man was obviously agog to have Christophe standing so close. Twice he broke off what he was doing to Phoebe and approached Christophe, once with a comb and once with a brush, but both times he changed his mind at the last moment. There was no need to touch Christophe. Nothing could be done to improve on perfection.

Phoebe's new haircut looked surprisingly good. She'd been

afraid she might end up with blue or pink stripes, but they left her color natural. When the clothes shopping began, things got even more amazing. They were met by a representative of French Vogue and taken to a private salon in a beautiful limestone mansion on rue de la Paix. Stylists from the major fashion houses and boutiques descended on Phoebe and brought *everything*—not just slacks and blouses, but undergarments, shoes, coats, hats, and bags.

Christophe explained that *couture* came from the word that meant to sew and told Phoebe, as if he was talking to a small child, that clothes looked better if the sewing happened after you were measured, rather than before you arrived. He said it wasn't good to purchase from a store and try to make yourself fit inside whatever they already had hanging around.

Phoebe pointed out that he was wearing off the rack Levis and a Hanes t-shirt.

"Some people are naturally made in the sizes the designers know look the best."

He said he wanted her to get a well-rounded understanding of fashion, so he had invited houses from several nations to assist her— Christian Marie Marc Lacroix from France, Cristobal Balenciaga from Spain, and Valentino Garavani from Italy.

Hermes and Gucci had some wonderful things, Christophe conceded, but they began as saddle makers and this should never be forgotten. Some of the pieces were specially-made prototypes presented to Christophe by designers for his opinion. Should they go in this direction? What did he think?

Phoebe had very little say about any of it. She was worried that she would end up looking ridiculous, but of course she didn't. Christophe selected only classic pieces that made Phoebe look elegant for the first time in her life. And the tweaks by the tailors worked magic. This was indeed the secret to looking good and feeling comfortable, custom fittings.

What a day. The sacred and the profane. The pinnacle of each, back-to-back.

It was like shopping, in reverse. They acquired box after box of amazing things without the need to go anywhere or pay for any of it. *No please, just take it. It would be such an honor to have your friend wearing our humble offerings.* Despite what Christophe said about them being jumped up saddle makers, Hermes was Phoebe's favorite store. The pleated scarf and shawl displays in the window at 24 rue Fauberg St. Honore were positioned around antique samurai armor in which the countless tiny plates were held together with hundreds of exquisite ribbons. Phoebe was moved to tears, yet again.

"Culture is man's way of reflecting back up to God what it is like to be here on the earth. Every culture has different gifts," said Christophe, as he watched Phoebe's longing perusal of the Hermes silks. "Each makes a different artistic contribution. The talent of the French is *style*. Your genetic line is from Scotland. Scotland is not known for its fashion."

"You mean because the men wear skirts and carry pocketbooks made from dead badgers?" Phoebe asked. "It's humiliating to admit it here, on the sidewalk in front of Hermes, but my primary fashion objective for the previous three decades has been to wear clothes that look don't look any worse with blood or vomit on em."

She wondered about Christophe. Which culture's gift to the world was the Lord of Blondness. "Where are you from?" she asked.

"My genetic line is from Denmark."

He's a Great Dane, Phoebe thought, struggling not to laugh. She felt a little bit sorry for him. It must be hard to be from a country that was famous for a deranged verbose prince and bad pastry, neither of which actually originated there.

When her whirlwind makeover was concluded, Phoebe said, "I've never seen such groveling worship of one human by so many others."

"They cannot help themselves," Christophe said.

"Maybe *you* should help them."

"If I did that, they would go from happiness to sadness—and you would not have anything to wear tomorrow."

Phoebe looked at all the boxes and bags. In France, the containers were as beautiful as the contents. They'd walked past a sidewalk display of fresh vegetables where she'd almost swooned when she saw bundles of asparagus tied with purple silk ribbon in a bow. "What're we gonna do with all this stuff?"

"The overflow is kept at *Le Seigneur's*. We often need to travel on short notice, and this way we can pack quickly."

It was getting dark. Finally, the longest day of the year was nearly over. Christophe told Phoebe that they were tasked with picking up a *voyant* for the return trip. Phoebe had no idea what that was, but learned that it meant a seer. "Are you a *voyant*?" Phoebe asked.

"No," Christophe said.

"You're a mind reader, though. You've done it to me several times."

"No one is allowed to read another's thoughts literally. That gift is not given to anyone. We are protected from each other in that way. The downside of this is that people get tortured for information.

"But if we are still, open, reserve subjective reactions or judgment, and cultivate a deep interior silence, we can sense the movements of each other's souls, especially if we are in close proximity to them. That is what real intimacy is, spiritual intimacy."

"But what about all the psychics you hear about? Some of them can know things about other people that are obviously true, things that the rest of us wouldn't have been able to know."

"You will enjoy our passenger," he said, "She can explain these things to you on the return flight."

According to Christophe the individual they were to take back with them had become aware of significant impending events and been given a message from the spiritual world that needed to be discussed with *Le Seigneur* in person.

When they arrived at the Ritz to make the pickup, Phoebe discovered the seer was a glamorous lady named Caterina Abatangelo, who had to be in her seventies at least. The lady looked her age and was beautiful. Her most striking assets were her cheekbones, aristocratic nose, and a beautifully styled luxuriant mane of pure white hair. She reminded Phoebe of the legendary high fashion model Carmen dell'Orefice who was still working in her eighties.

Caterina and Christophe exchanged the ritual of four kisses

that Christophe had assured her was the correct way to greet friends in France. Left cheek, right cheek, then repeat. The magnificence of the hair swishing during that kiss was sufficient to stop traffic throughout Place Vendome.

As she was getting into the car that would take them to the airport, Caterina took Phoebe's hand. Then she looked up in surprise. She waited until Phoebe was seated next to her in the back, with Christophe and the driver in the front, then Caterina leaned over and whispered, "I realize this will sound silly, but I am quite serious. You will soon become involved with a tall dark stranger. *Several of them* in fact," she said smiling and wiggling her elegant eyebrows. Then she tightened her grip on Phoebe's hand and leaned even closer to whisper softly into her ear, "And one blond."

DEDICATION

A big thank you to Fred Frishe for his scholarship and insights into the relationship between tariffs and the American Civil War; and also for his genuinely riveting tours of Cleveland, *The Mistake on the Lake*.

I am grateful to Austin Faulkner, M.D. for information about the PACS system. Thanks to Gary Turner for information on high-end private jets and flights to France, fellow authors Leighann Dobbs, Adriana Koulias, and Louisa Locke for their advice, and Margaret Moore and Kim Franklin for helpful edits.

Many thanks to Joyce Reilly for taking me all over New York, New Jersey, and Connecticut in high style, to the Frick twice, and especially for putting up with me bursting into tears each time I walked by the portrait of Sir Thomas More. I particularly appreciate her company at Biltmore, madcap sense of humor, and superb driving skills in New York City.

I am deeply grateful to Sandra Johanson, Ph.D. for her friendship, for putting up with my zany struggle to publish *Bear in the Back Seat* from her kitchen island (which was successful enough to make a #9 *Wall Street Journal* best seller), and for letting me stay with her, once during a blizzard when the power was out for days, forcing us to go to the Short Hills Mall to get warm. I'm pretty sure

Hurricane Sandy was named for her.

Thanks to Bran Rogers for artistic guidance, Brian Pittman for architectural advice, John Plummer for four free tickets to Biltmore, and Janey and Brian Newton for a wonderfully peaceful place to get a first draft of this book completed.

And a big thank you to Courtney Lix for her expert editorial suggestions and for (accidentally) setting me off on a path of writing fiction.

RESEARCH RESOURCES

The venerable and awe-inspiring history of the real Mystery Schools through the ages is detailed in two superb books: *The Great Initiates: A Study of the Secret History of Religions*, by Edouard Schure, and *An Endless Trace: The Passionate Pursuit of Wisdom in the West*, by Christopher Bamford.

Historical details about the Mystery School at Chartres are described in *The Golden Age of Chartres: The Teachings of a Mystery School and the Eternal Feminine*, by Rene M. Querido.

A superb version of *O Magnum Mysterium* by the Nordic Chamber Choir singing the M. Lauridsen arrangement is available at https://www.youtube.com/watch?v=nn5ken3RJBo

OTHER BOOKS
BY CAROLYN JOURDAN

Jourdan's memoir, *Heart in the Right Place,* is a *Wall Street Journal* Bestseller (#7 in the nation) and #1 on Amazon in Biography, Memoir, Medicine, and Science. It is on hundreds of lists of best books of the year, best book club books, and funniest books. It was chosen as *Family Circle* magazine's first ever Book of the Month and won the *Elle* magazine Reader's Prize.

"Heartwarming, funny and utterly appealing." **Fannie Flagg** -- Author of *Fried Green Tomatoes*

"This is a wonderful book. I would have enjoyed it even if Carolyn wasn't a neighbor of mine in East Tennessee. She is a great writer." **Dolly Parton** -- Singer, Songwriter, and Actress

Medicine Men: Extreme Appalachian Doctoring reached #1 on all of Amazon Kindle! It was also #1 in Non-Fiction, Biography, Memoir, Medicine, Science, and Doctor-Patient Relations.

Bear in the Back Seat: Adventures of a Wildlife Ranger in the Great Smoky Mountains National Park, Volume 1 is a *Wall Street Journal* Bestseller (#9 in the nation).

Bear in the Back Seat II continues the national bestselling memoir of Kim DeLozier, Wildlife Ranger.

Jourdan's previous mystery, *Out on a Limb,* was ranked #1 in Medical Fiction, #1 Mystery, and #1 Cozy Mystery on Amazon. Reviewers describe this cozy, scientific, medical mystery as "No. 1 Ladies Detective Agency of the Great Smoky Mountains", "CSI Meets Animal Planet", and "An Appalachian Michael Crichton."

ABOUT THE AUTHOR

Carolyn is a former U.S. Senate Counsel to the Committee on Environment and Public Works and the Committee on Governmental Affairs. She has degrees from the University of Tennessee in Biomedical Engineering and Law. Carolyn lives on the family farm in Strawberry Plains, Tennessee, with many stray animals. She is a popular speaker on television, radio, and in person.

www.ingramcontent.com/pod-product-compliance
Lightning Source LLC
Chambersburg PA
CBHW060129130626
46556CB00006B/2286